BAD BOYS DO IT *Better*

4

In Love With an Outlaw

A NOVEL BY

PORSCHA STERLING

I need a gangsta
To love me better
Than all the others do

To always forgive me
Ride or die with me
That's just what gangsters do

- Kehlani

Previously...

Janelle

"*D*on't leave out the hotel," Luke told me, and I rolled my eyes. Here he was with the rules again.

"I'm serious, Nell. You got massages, food and all kinds of shit you can order in this hotel. Don't leave out until I get back."

"Yeeeeesss, sirrrrrr," I droned, rolling over in the bed.

I was sore as hell. Especially between my legs. It was the next morning, and Luke and I had spent most of the night before 'practicing for babies' as he called it. Thank God I was on the pill or I would be pregnant with triplets. Luke's sexual appetite was always on one hundred, and it was hard for me to keep up sometimes because he literally seemed to rub my insides raw. But then I remembered all the nasty bitches who would love to take my place and got my act together.

Today was the day that Luke and his brothers did whatever the hell they were in town to do—of which I still had no details. Maybe it was the lawyer in me but I was dying to know what was going on, however, Luke knew how to keep a secret and wouldn't let a single thing slip. So I just left it alone.

"Remember when you put things on the room, don't sign in your name. *We* aren't here… according to the hotel, your name is Joyce Robertson."

"You could've gave us some better names, James Robertson," I told him, using his fake name with a roll of my eyes.

"Whatever. Just enjoy bein' my Mrs." He kissed me on my forehead and started towards the door with a bag in his hand.

My heart fluttered at him saying that I was his Mrs.…even if he was being facetious. My emotions were crazy because I kept telling myself that it wasn't time to be pressing Luke for a ring. I hadn't even thought about wanting a ring until Teema and Kane became engaged. But now, ever since they announced they were getting married, it was all that was on my mind. I'd been stung by the marriage bug.

"Don't forget what I said, Janelle," Luke warned me one last time before leaving the room.

"Yeah, yeah, yeah," I told him and waved him away.

After he left, I rolled over to get a little more sleep since I hadn't slept much at all the night before but was awakened about an hour later to my phone blaring in my ear.

"Hello?"

"Jani, do you know what's going on with Carm?" It was Mixie and she sounded way too worried for this early in the morning.

"No, I haven't talked to her in about a week or so. Why? What's going on?"

"Well…she's home."

That got my attention. Blinking a few times, I sat up in the bed and gripped the phone even closer to my ear.

"What do you mean she's home? Daddy let her come back?"

"Yeah…she's living back home now. She spoke to Daddy, but they've been all top-secret about what happened and why she's here."

I grabbed my owl necklace and squeezed tightly on it, not knowing why my heart was throbbing in my chest. I guess because I missed my daddy so much, but he still didn't care to see me but had seemingly welcomed Carmella with open arms.

"Has Daddy called you at all?" Mixie asking that question only made the throbbing pain in my chest even stronger and more painful.

"No."

"Have you tried to call him?"

"Yes." That admission brought tears to my eyes.

"He'll come around, Janelle. I promise he will. He loves you."

A few tears rolled down my cheeks, and I wiped them away. Mixie and I shared a few words of small talk, but I knew that she was only trying to make me feel better about being Daddy's only daughter that he refused to see, and then we hung up the phone. I laid in the bed crying for what felt like hours before I decided that I needed a pick-me-up. I needed to get to the spa and get my relaxation on. Reaching over to the nightstand, I picked up the spa card and nearly fainted when I saw the price list of activities. Thankfully, I had a man with a black card who had given me full access so I was free to do everything I could dream of.

"Hello, how may I help you?" The spa clerk answered the phone with a French accent that made me wonder if it was authentic or fake.

"Hi, I would like to order a few spa treatments for the day," I started before rattling down everything I wanted to try out and then some extra for good measure.

The clerk happily repeated everything that I wanted, as if she would be getting paid a percentage of the cost just for taking the order, and then told me to head on down in an hour. I was there fifteen minutes early. So much had happened in my life within the past few weeks, and I needed this.

Four hours later, I was a new woman. Rose petal baths, warm pumpkin and aloe facials, and a deep tissue massage could do that type of thing to you. I was floating on cloud nine all the way until I got to the register.

"I'm sorry, we are going to need an ID for us to charge the card on file," the spa clerk stated.

Blinking a few times, I frowned and stared right back at her. "Why? I haven't needed to show my ID for anything else that I've charged to the room."

"It's because of the price. Our hotel has a policy that anything over $2,000 requires proper ID," she replied, and I could've sworn I heard her lil' fake ass accent falter a bit. She was a fake.

"Well, I don't have my ID," I told her, knowing damn well that no driver's license I had said 'Joyce Robertson.' Can I just have my husband come settle this when he gets back? He should have cash."

The bitch gave me a look that said everything her mouth didn't say. I knew she was calling me all kinds of 'niggas' and 'bitches' right then.

"We require payment as soon as the services are rendered. We have an ATM on the first floor that you are free to use to get the money…if you have it."

I wanted to slap the shit out of her. So there it was; she felt like I was as much of a fraud as she was with her fake ass accent.

"I *do* have the money, but I'm pretty sure that I can't deduct $2,000 out of the damn ATM," I said, waving my debit card in the air angrily.

With a straight face, she offered me another alternative.

"That bank that matches your card is two blocks away. Any of our courtesy drivers can take you there. I apologize, but without proper ID, we can't run the card on file. It's a security protocol the hotel uses to keep *our patrons* safe."

The way she said it pissed me off. Like I was an imposter that didn't belong in the building. The only thing stopping me from slapping the shit out of her was because I didn't want to cause a scene that would have Luke cussing me out later after he bailed me out of jail.

"Fine, I'll go to the bank."

"Mercedes will lead you to the courtesy driver," the clerk added, and I rolled my eyes. The only reason Mercedes was leading me anywhere was not because she was being nice, but to make sure I didn't run off somewhere without paying. This was some bullshit. The whole reason for the massage was to relax and as soon as I got out, these assholes were stressing me out.

I stomped into the bank mad as hell. Not only was I being made to withdraw money out of my account when I shouldn't have had to, I had to ride the entire way to the bank with the stank ass courtesy driver who smelled like old cheese grits. I swear I felt like I was going to vomit the entire way to the bank, it was so disgusting.

"Welcome, how can I help you?"

"Hi," I began, huffing as I lay on the counter. "I need to withdraw $2,356 from my checking account. Big bills are fine for the two grand."

I read off the exact amount of the spa bill without adding any for tip. They could miss me on that because I'd be damned if I paid them anything extra. My tip would be to tell their asses to get their shit together so that high paying customers like me didn't have to take a fuckin' stank ass car two blocks to the bank to pay a bill.

"Here you go, Ms. Pickney. Let me count this out for you. One, two, three, four—"

"Everybody get on the fuckin' floor! Hug the fuckin' floor right now!"

Pow! Pow! Pow!

Absolute chaos erupted around me and, without even thinking, I obeyed the orders that were given and hugged the ground. People were screaming, some were praying and others were crying, but my only thought was that I had to think.

"Get on the fuckin' ground! And keep your eyes down!" the robotic voice said again.

My head was too close to the ground to see anything, but I could hear a collection of feet running about, demanding different things from the bank tellers and staff.

"Grab one of them muthafuckas and bring 'em in the back," another one said, speaking through whatever instrument they were all using to disguise their voices.

Squeezing my eyes closed, I prayed to the Lord that whoever they chose to grab wouldn't be me, but the reality was, I'd already had a fucked up day, and me being the one they chose to make a hostage would only be icing on the cake. Sure enough, while I had my face pressed to the ground, praying to Jesus to shed a little grace on me, I felt my body being plucked off the floor by my arms.

"Get da fuck up. Keep your head down!"

Tears burned in my eyes, but I did as I was told. When I worked at the clinic, we were often drilled on the proper procedures to take if we were robbed. Since we had a little bit of change and were in the pit of the ghetto, it was a risk of working there, but it never happened while I was employed. Now here I was trying to drudge up the memories of what I'd been told to do. The only rule I could remember vividly was to always comply with the robber's demands. Never play the hero. Shit, I couldn't play the hero if I tried. I was scared to death. I felt like I was about to piss my pants.

"I got the hostage. We good to go, fam," the man holding on to me said as he roughly pulled me into a room. His fingers were pressed so hard into my arm that it hurt, and I winced in pain.

"Move another fuckin' muscle and I'll fuckin' put a hot one in your brain, bitch!"

The next thing I felt was metal to my head, and tears began to stream down my eyes. I was gonna die.

Oh God, please! Don't let me die like this. God, please! I screamed within my mind.

Although my head was down, I heard movement in the room and I knew that there were many other people there. One was a woman and she was crying pretty hard. I assumed she was a hostage just like me.

"Stop all that fuckin' cryin' and open the fuckin' safe up. Now, before I blow your fuckin' brains out!"

"Or do you want us to blow her brains out and let you watch?" the man holding me asked with a teasing tone that could be heard through the robotic voice disguise. I let out a loud sob, unable to play the strong one anymore.

"Right…actually, I think that's a good idea," another one said. "If you don't get your shit together and open this shit in the next few seconds, we'll blast a hole in…OH SHIT!"

The room went silent except for the woman's sobs, and the hairs rose up on my arm as I got the crazy feeling that all eyes were on me.

"Get that fuckin' gun from her head, yo," one of them said.

"Huh?" the man holding me asked, gripping me even harder. "What da fuck you—"

"I said put da fuckin' gun down, now!"

Instantly, the gun was pulled from my head and I let out a deep breath. Then there was silence in the room.

Something seemed off.

Against my better judgment, I looked up even though I knew that was a rule that I was breaking. You were never supposed to look them in their eyes or look at them at all, for fear that you would make yourself a witness to their identity and cost your life. But there was something about this situation that seemed peculiar to me, and I found myself breaking the rules. When I lifted my head, my eyes fell first on the one who had yelled for my captor to move the gun from my head, and I froze.

He was covered from head to toe in army fatigue as well as a mask on his face, and I couldn't see any of his skin... nothing but the white of his eyes. But that was enough. I knew the man I loved when I saw him.

"Luke!"

He lifted his hand, but I could tell I'd done something wrong by the way the tallest one in the room stiffened up. Luke's eyes went to him and I saw him let out a breath. His shoulders slumped and I tried to realize what I'd done wrong. It only took a few seconds of racking my brain before I got it.

Fuck! I said his name!

"Shit," another one said. I didn't recognize who it was and his voice was disguised.

"It's open," the woman who had been working on the safe said with a shaky voice, and one of the other men pulled her aggressively away from the opening as another one filed in. My eyes were still on Luke. The man I thought I knew better than I knew myself. I was learning that there was more to learn. And I was about to get my first lesson.

"Y'all four go get everything so we can get out of this bitch. Luke... you responsible for this fuck up so I'll leave you to handle it."

He walked away and I backed into a corner, wondering what was meant by that statement.

"Nell, turn around," he said and my knees started knocking.

Oh god... he wasn't going to kill me, was he? I didn't know the rules of the street or what happened when things like this happened. Was I the fuck up that needed to be handled?

"I'm sorry, I—"

"Turn around!" he ordered with force, and I did as I was told. I wanted to cry, but I was afraid beyond tears. Squeezing my eyes closed, I waited for death to come.

"Please... please, no!"

Zip! Zip!

The sound of something heavy dropping to the ground was the next sound I heard. With my knees still knocking against each other and my bottom lip quivering, I turned around slowly. The first thing I saw was the bank employee sprawled out on the ground with a perfectly round hole in her head and another in her chest. I felt weak and I nearly fell onto the floor, using only a metal beam on the wall to steady myself from hitting the floor.

Tears fell but they didn't block out the image of Luke walking towards me. I couldn't see his face, but I didn't need to in order to feel his anger. And there was no mistaking it. All of it was aimed at me.

"I said this one time and I'm goin' to say the shit again... hopefully for the last muthafuckin' time," Luke gritted through his teeth. "Let this be the *last* fuckin' time you don't listen to me."

I sunk to the ground and dropped my head in my hands, sobbing uncontrollably.

"FUCK!" Luke yelled, making me jump. "Let's get da fuck out of here. We got 30 seconds to leave."

"We need to get her?" someone asked.

"No," Luke replied back. Even though he still had on the voice disguise, I could still hear the fury in his tone. "Leave her there. Let's go."

And I stayed there... right where he'd left me. I was still sitting in that same spot, long after the footsteps were gone and even when I began to hear the sirens approaching. My heart was so tight in my chest that I felt like I was going to have a heart attack. I was scared out of my mind, in the room with the woman Luke had murdered because of my own stupidity, and worst of all, Luke had abandoned me.

If this was what it meant to be in love with an outlaw, I wasn't sure if it was what I really wanted.

Janelle

"*H*ave you heard from him yet?"

"No."

"So, basically, we all nigga-less," Sidney surmised, rolling her eyes. "Except for Faviola's hoe ass. What the hell is up with that?"

Scrunching up her nose, Faviola looked at Sidney and frowned. "I'm not a hoe anymore, Sid. I've had 'hoe days.' It's a difference. Now I'm in a committed relationship with my man."

After saying her piece, she leaned down and continued polishing her toenails some lime green color to match her new lime green wig. I didn't really care for Faviola as a person—she was much too ratchet and over the top for me—but one thing I could say is that she was definitely her own person. I loved the part of her that felt comfortable being who she was without a care in the world about what others thought. I could learn something from her.

We were all in Sidney's new place, helping her unpack a few things. She was trying to escape Yolo and was pretty much building a new life so that he couldn't contact her. She quit her job, moved out of her old place with Faviola and even changed her phone number. I still didn't know what happened between them, but it had to be serious because Sidney seemed officially fed up.

"When's the last time you spoke to him?"

"I haven't seen him since he got mad at me… while we were on vacation," I replied, making sure to be coy about what I did. Sidney let it go, probably because she wasn't telling us much about what happened between her and Yolo either, but Faviola went straight in for the kill.

"Well, bitch, what did you do? From what I've seen about Outlaw and how you've had him wrapped around your lil' finger, it must have been some big time shit!"

I shook my head and grabbed up the ice macchiato I'd been sipping. "I just did something stupid. It wasn't really my fault though, but he won't speak to me. He took a different flight back and by the time I got to his apartment, he wasn't there and a lot of his things were gone."

"Damn," Sidney replied and sucked her teeth. "I've known Outlaw to be in his feelings about shit before, but usually it doesn't last all that long."

"It's been a week," I sulked, willing myself not to cry.

A whole week and I hadn't seen him or heard a word from him. At the same time, it wasn't like I'd been trying. On one hand, I missed Luke and wanted things to be how they were. But, on the other hand, he'd killed someone in front of me. I'd gotten an up-close look at what it was that he and his brothers were capable of, and it didn't sit well with me.

To know that someone was responsible for heinous crimes and to see them commit them were two different things. After Luke left me at the bank, I had to be questioned by police. I saw them bag up the body of the woman who had been shot because of me, and I also had to worry about whether or not I'd blown Luke's cover by having my name on the police records. He'd done so much to make sure that we arrived here without a trace, and in a couple hours, I messed that up for the both of us.

"Give it some time," Sidney replied with a shrug. "The Murray brothers are never mad for long. Especially not the youngest ones. Yolo and Outlaw don't know how to hold a damn grudge."

"Speaking of Yolo, his ass still blowing up my phone," Faviola said with a hint of a chuckle but kept her eyes on her toes.

"Block his ass," was all Sidney said, and even I had to lift my brows. Faviola's head shot up.

"You're sure you're done with him like that?"

"Yes," she replied with ease, as she pulled another box towards her to open it up. "Block him. I can't deal with him anymore."

Silence hung in the air as we all thought about our man problems; all of us with solemn looks on our faces except for Faviola who, for once, had everything going right in her life. After losing the baby, she and Tank seemed to be closer than ever and were in an official relationship, by the looks of it. It was so crazy how things had changed so much in a matter of weeks.

"What's going on with Carm?" Sidney asked, and an immediate frown crossed my face. I hadn't heard from my sister in weeks and even after speaking with Mixie and Vonia, I was no closer to knowing what was going on with her. They said that Daddy hadn't opened his mouth to say anything about what she was up to other than that 'she needs your prayers.' What the hell did that mean?

"I don't know. Last I heard, she was back home but my daddy and I aren't talking, and he hasn't told my other sisters anything about what she's up to."

"You think she in the witness protection program? Like she witnessed some shit in the porn business that can get her popped so your daddy tryin' to hide her ass to keep her safe?"

Cutting my eyes at Faviola, I almost frowned at the thirsty ass look on her face. She was ready for some good ass gossip. Now that her life was dry of it, she needed something to fill the void.

"No, it's not that… I'm just hoping she didn't get herself into some trouble out here."

"So you haven't heard anything at all?"

I shook my head and was about to say something, but I looked at Sidney who glanced at Faviola in a way that gave me pause. They exchanged knowing glances, making me curious about what they were thinking. Before I could even ask, Sidney started to talk.

"Janelle, Carm had a little addiction she was dealin' with."

"Addiction?" I parroted and my neck jerked back. I looked back and forth between them, waiting for one of them to say they were kidding or it wasn't exactly what I was thinking, but Faviola just dropped her head back down to her toes and commenced to polishing them.

"Yeah, she was on that white girl. Not too bad at first, but the last couple times I hung with her, I could tell she was in a little deep and I mentioned it to Cree. You hadn't noticed from being around her?"

I pulled my lips into my mouth and looked down, embarrassed to admit that I'd been hanging with Carmella in person less and less since making things official with Luke. She'd been involved in her life and I was wrapped up in mine, thinking that she was too busy being boo'ed up with Cree to be around me as much as she'd been before. I didn't think anything of it but now to know that she was using drugs—cocaine of *all* drugs—made me feel like a shitty sister. How was it that Sidney and Faviola knew but I didn't?

"I don't know if that's the reason she went home, but from how your dad is actin' and you not being able to get in contact with her... it seems like he probably got her ass in rehab," Sidney finished, and I tried to push away the tears that came to my eyes.

The main thing that was messing with me was that, of all people, I hadn't been there for her and I was in the same damn city. As the oldest, I'd always been there for my sisters, but I was hearing what Carmella was going through from some chicks who had only known her a few months in comparison to me, who had known her for her entire life. Couple that with the fact that I was crying and shit over a man who had murdered someone then left me, *and* the fact that I was jobless after leaving the job I'd dreamed my whole life for... I didn't know who I was anymore. I didn't know who I was becoming. I definitely wasn't the same responsible and predictable Janelle from before.

What the hell was going on with my life?

Outlaw

"*I*t's about time you come to see me, boy!"

Lifting one brow, I looked over at my grandmother as she stood at the entrance of the kitchen with her hands on her hips, wearing one of the things I loved to see her in: an apron. That meant it was some good ass food on the way. Or, from the smell of it, some good ass food was almost done.

"You know I always come over to see my ole girl; don't act like that."

Before she got a chance to say anything, I walked into the kitchen and started peeking in the pots. She had some good ass greens on the stove, yellow rice and macaroni and cheese in the oven, along with some crispy fried chicken. Yeah, I was chilling in BK for the moment, but I was nothing but a country ass nigga at heart and I damn sure ate like one.

"You betta had washed them nasty ass hands. I don't know where they been! Especially since you got a lil' girlfriend but still ain't brought her over to meet me yet."

I heard the hurt in her tone even though she hid it well. It was true though. As close as Janelle and I had gotten, I still hadn't bothered to bring her over to meet my grandmother. I had a reason for that though. Other than Sidney, no woman who has ran into my grandmother has been able to put up with her ass. In her mind, nobody was good enough for her grandsons, and she made sure to give any woman hell who threatened to take a place in our lives. I wasn't ready to deal with the drama yet when it came to Janelle. And now it looked like I didn't have to.

"We ain't on good terms right now," I informed her, as I poured myself a big cup of kool-aid and washed it down in only a few gulps. When I lowered the cup from my lips, she was staring right at me.

"Not on good terms, huh? Is that why you look like a lil' ole lost puppy?"

I frowned at her and dropped the cup in the sink. "What you mean?"

She pressed her lips firmly together and eyed me as I walked over and dropped down onto the couch, sitting directly across from her. Pulling my fitted from off the top of my head, I ran my hand over my head before replacing it back on top of my braids and letting out a loud sigh. I didn't come over to her house to have to deal with my issues with Janelle. I'd come over here to escape them. It was lonely as hell sitting in a house by myself thinking about the one woman who I wanted to spend my time with, but I couldn't bring myself to correct that. Janelle had fucked up bad and her fuck up became mine.

Since what happened during our last job, I hadn't spoken to Kane once and I wasn't trying to make a change to that either. I knew that he was ready to put his foot in my ass and I couldn't even blame him. We had rules for a reason. They were to protect us from getting caught up but more and more I saw myself breaking the rules for Janelle. Of all my brothers, Kane was the angriest about this because he had more to lose. He now had a daughter and a soon-to-be wife that he had to take care of and be there for. My mistakes could land us all in lock up for the rest of our lives. The shit was serious and because of that, I had to get my head right. I couldn't do that with Janelle around.

"Look at you! You came over here looking like somebody shot your favorite dog. You got them raggedy ass braids on your head, looking like they ain't been done in weeks. Your face long as hell… I'm surprised you're not walking on your chin right now." She grunted out what sounded like a dry chuckle and then crossed her arms in front of her chest as she sat back in her seat. "The only time I seen a man look like that is when he havin' woman problems. So what happened?"

I looked right at her but didn't say a word. It wasn't in me to explain the decisions I made about my life to anyone, my grandmother included. Besides, there wasn't anything she could do to help the situation out. My stance on everything wasn't changing. I was about to tell her that when something new above her fireplace caught my attention.

"What the hell you got a white ass Jesus on your fireplace for, grandma? Since when you religious anyways?" I asked her with bended brow and a hint of a smile on my lips.

"What you mean, boy? I always been holy and holding on to my religion," she replied as if it was a matter of fact, and pulled her silk shawl tight around her shoulders to cover her cleavage.

Holy, my ass.

"They ain't have no black Jesus where you bought this one at

19

though?" I continued to tease her, knowing I was about to strike a nerve.

"It don't matter the color of Jesus, boy! Just as long as we serve Him and Him alone!"

She was about two seconds away from thumping me in the head with the Bible she probably had tucked somewhere, so I just left her alone and shook my head. The very next second, my thoughts were back on Janelle, thinking about the day that she was walking home from church and I ran up on her talking to some random nigga after ignoring my calls. The memory brought a hint of a smile to my face, but it was wiped away just as quickly when I thought about how I hadn't seen or heard from her in a minute. I missed her ass but I needed to teach her a lesson. This shit I was involved in was serious, and I didn't have room for her to go against the things I told her to do.

"That's not the subject we were on anyways. We were talkin' about you and this lil' lady who got you lookin' how you lookin'. I know you, Luke, and if this lil' girl got you all worked up like this, maybe it's a good thing the lil' heffa gone somewhere. She was probably bad news anyways."

"She wasn't bad news," I corrected her, unable to keep myself from defending Janelle. "She's just ain't from the streets so she gotta make adjustments to be with a nigga like me."

"And you have to make adjustments to be with a woman like her," my grandmother chimed in, and I realized then that she'd been able to sucker me into saying more than I wanted to say. "You're stubborn but bein' with a woman like you just described will require a whole lot of patience from you. If you not willing to be patient with her, the same way you expect her to be with you, then you'll lose her. And that's what your ass gets."

With a satisfied smirk on her face, she sat back in her chair and turned to look out the window. My brows lifted and I glanced at the white Jesus on the wall, but I didn't say nothing about her cursing at a nigga even though she was supposed to be holy now. Standing up, I walked over to the front door, deciding that I no longer wanted to stay for dinner. I had too much on my mind at the moment, and the last thing I was thinking about was eating.

"You leavin'?" my grandmother asked, and I nodded my head before doubling back to give her a kiss on the cheek. She patted me on the back and then started to hum to herself as I left.

"I'll call her," was the last thing I said before closing the door behind me.

It was time to stop with the games. I knew I wanted to be with Janelle... I'd begged her to choose me over her father, her career and just about everything else in her life. The least I could do was make sure that she knew she'd made the right decision by choosing to be with a nigga like me.

Sidney

*Y*olo not being in my life had me all fucked up.

I wouldn't admit it to anyone but the ones closest to me could see that it was true. I wasn't the same Sid anymore. The perfect example of that was the fact that I was still in the damn bed, sleeping my life away when it was nearly 2 o'clock in the afternoon on a Saturday. I didn't want to admit it, but I was depressed and trying to hide from, not only Yolo, but the world. My savings were dwindling to nothing, but I wasn't even pressed about finding a new job. Outside of laying up in the bed, sleeping the days away or stuffing my face full of junk food, I wasn't doing a damn thing with my life.

Knock, knock, knock!

Groaning, I pulled the pillow over my head and wished away whoever it was at the door. I didn't want company and that should have been evident from the fact that I'd been ignoring everyone's calls. But the knocking continued on relentlessly. Whoever it was at the door was adamant about not being ignored.

How do they even know I am home? I didn't have a car and all of the lights in my apartment were definitely turned off. But why hadn't they left by now?

"Okay! I'm coming!" I growled as I rose out of the bed, kicking the sheets from my legs.

Thankfully, one of the few things I'd been able to accomplish the past few days was washing my ass so I at least looked decent... never mind that my hair was tossed all over my head and matted to show proof of the fact that I hadn't combed it in days. It was half straight and half curly—basically, it looked like a bird's nest.

"Who is it?" I asked before reaching the door, even though I knew that it could only be about a handful of people. I'd only told a few about this place, mainly just the friends who helped me move. I didn't even tell my mama about my new address because I knew that Yolo had her wrapped around his finger. Anything she knew about my whereabouts, she would let him know about immediately and convince herself that it was for my own good.

"Mike! Open up!"

Sighing, I ran to the nearest mirror and at least tried to run my fingers through my hair. Mike, my former co-worker, had been one of the ones to help me move a lot of my furniture into my new place, and he was also one of the ones blowing up my damn phone nearly every day since I'd moved in. It made sense that he was worried about me; he seemed to regard me as his little sister. That was one reason why I wasn't too bothered to change out of the tiny ass pajama shorts I had on or actually grab a real comb to run through my head. In my mind, he was fam.

Rolling my eyes, I pulled open the door and breathed out a quick 'Hey' to Mike before stepping to the side to let him in. He paused, his smile frozen on his face, until his eyes dipped down to my attire: a sheer white spaghetti strap top and silk, booty short pajamas. Even with my disheveled appearance, I caught the look in his eyes and it surprised me to see something there that I hadn't expected. Immediately, I felt the need to change out of what I was wearing and tugged at the hem of my shorts as I backed out of the way.

"Um… you can come in and sit down. I'm going to go change," I told him, as I ambled backwards from him, awkwardly trying to delay the moment where I would need to turn my back to him and expose my ass, so I could walk down the hall to my room.

Mike, sensing my discomfort, averted his attention long enough for me to turn and run down the hall, but for some reason, I still felt like once my back was fully turned, his eyes were on me.

"Whoa," I mumbled to myself as soon as I was in my room with the door safely closed behind me.

Mike and I had been friends for a while, but I'd never gotten the vibe that he was attracted to me in any way. Part of that could be the fact that I spent most of that time dressed in the same exact things he wore, and part of that could be because I'd never seen him with a woman or heard him mention one so I assumed he was gay. Either way, I'd built it up in my mind that he was more like the older brother I'd never had than anything else. Apparently, he didn't see me as his little sister.

After changing into some sweatpants and a t-shirt and then tugging my hair into a messy ponytail, I walked back into the living room, feeling much different around Mike than I'd ever felt before. Still, I tried to keep my cool and pretend like nothing had changed between us.

"What's up, bruh?" I said and then got the feeling that I was trying a little too hard to go back to being regarded as 'one of the boys.' "I mean, what's... going on with you?"

"You haven't been answering my calls so I wanted to make sure you were good. I even called Faviola but she said she hadn't heard from you either."

Hearing him state that he'd called Faviola made me lift a brow and stare at him for a minute. Now I knew his ass had to be desperate because he didn't like Faviola at all. Like with most people, she was just too much for him with all her drama and ratchet ways. In the middle of staring at him, I couldn't help but notice that he was letting his hair grow out a little as well as his beard. Mike had always been attractive, but I'd never seen him in the way I was seeing him now. I stirred in my seat and looked away. This shit was starting to get a little too uncomfortable.

"I just wanted some time to myself. I got a lot of shit changing in my life and I need to get a grasp on it and get myself together. I gotta find a job and—"

"I can help you with the job part," Mike cut in, quickly. "My cousin just opened his first bar and asked for my help with it. He'll need at least two good bartenders so... if you're interested."

The corners of Mike's mouth eased up into a half-smile and I ducked my head away from the look in his eyes and nodded my head, delivering a smile of my own.

"So we'll be workin' together again, huh?"

"I guess so," he replied.

"Well, give me all the details and tell me when to start… I'm there."

***

"The hell you got them tights on under that dress for? Take that shit off and let them legs show!"

Placing the glass in my hand on the top of the bar, I turned, cutting my eyes at Kyle, Mike's cousin. It was obvious that he was the type who believed a woman's body was part of the preferred ambiance of his club and wanted every woman in the building to have all her assets on blast. I wasn't feeling it. Even though I managed to toss off my Js, t-shirt and sweats for a dress and tights for my first day at work, it wasn't in me to be showing my ass for tips… even if that was what my new boss wanted.

"I'm not really cool with all that. I like to stay covered up for the most part," I told him, still cleaning the glasses to prepare for what was supposed to be a busy night.

"Leave her alone," Mike said, coming to my defense and earning a sideways look from his cousin. "Sid's not like these hoes you employ in here. She's not about to put her tits and ass on display to run up a check."

Kyle looked at him like it was a foreign concept to him that anybody wouldn't do anything for a check, before turning back to me.

"If you don't want to show some skin… your loss. Just don't come bitchin' to me later about my other girls out-tipping you."

And with that, he darted off, paying little attention to the ugly look that I was giving him. Close to where he had stood was another girl who worked there and had heard the entire conversation. She gave me a disgusted look with her nose high in the air, followed by a loud 'humph!' before walking away. I sighed and commenced to cleaning the glasses at the bar.

"Don't pay attention to him… or her," Mike added, coming up behind me. "Some people just don't understand that sometimes a little modesty goes a long way. Not every nigga wants a woman who got all her shit on display. Some of us want a lady."

With his final words, Mike slid his arm around my side and cupped his hand on my stomach, pulling me back into him. I was shocked but I didn't pull away. His scent seeped through my nostrils, putting me under a spell that traveled down to the crease between my thighs. I exhaled slowly, melting into him against my better judgment, until I realized that I'd lost my damn mind and snatched away.

"Thanks," I muttered, turning to face him and using the glass in my hand as a barrier between us.

Mike nodded his head and dropped his eyes away from my face for about a second. Then he looked back up with a new determination in his stare.

"Sid… I've been meaning to say that—"

"Hey, can I get a drink? Something special… and strong," a woman requested, sitting right in front of Mike.

I glanced at her, instantly noticing the flirty smile on her face and the way she straightened her back sharply to push up her breasts. This was always how it was with Mike—women were always attracted to him and would often spend more time at the bar trying to get his attention than actually entertaining the niggas who were buying the drinks. It was normal and never bothered me... before now.

"Something strong, huh?" Mike asked, playing his role that got him the big tips and flirting back at her. He leaned over the bar, into her face, and placed his elbows on the bar counter.

"Yeah and something sweet. Not too sweet though. I'm not scared if it's a little rough," she added, and I felt the urge to throw up.

Before I knew it, I caught myself rolling my eyes. I didn't realize I'd been caught until after Mike had walked away to prepare her drink.

"Uhm, you got a problem with your eyes?"

It took me a minute to realize that it was the thot referencing me. And then it took me another minute to remind myself that I needed this job and couldn't get fired on my first day.

"Naw, I'm good," was my only reply but I said it through gritted teeth.

"Excuse me," Mike said as he slid behind me, making a point to touch the space on my lower back, right above my ass. You know... that space that was specifically created on a woman's anatomy for men to caress and bring us to our knees. I felt a warmth there that lasted well after he'd removed his hand and was standing in front of the thirsty female to finish her drink.

"I think I got the perfect thing for you right here," Mike said and then poured the mixed drink in a glass before pushing it in front of the woman's face.

"Oh, I bet you do. You look like you can give me whatever it is I want."

Ugh, I swear vomit was about to spew from my lips. This was just sickening.

"I'm going to the restroom," I blurted out, tossing my towel on the bar counter.

I couldn't take this shit anymore! And I'd only been at work for about a half hour. How was I going to be able to deal with this night after night? I couldn't even deal for the rest of this night.

After sitting in the bathroom wasting as much time as I felt I could before Kyle came to look for me, I walked out, delighted to see that Mike's customer was gone and replaced by a man who wasn't paying him the least bit of attention.

"You okay?" Mike asked, his brow curled in concern. I nodded my head, pressed my lips together, but didn't say a word.

"She asked if you were my girlfriend," he said in a tone so low that I almost missed it. Jerking to attention, I snatched my head in his direction.

"Who?"

"The girl who was just here. Said she got a jealous vibe from you." He chuckled, but I felt my cheeks burn from embarrassment.

"Girlfriend? Jealous vibe? She must be already feelin' that lil' drink you gave her if she askin' stupid stuff like that. Not happenin'!" I started to laugh, not realizing that I may have gone a little overboard until I saw the hurt in Mike's eyes. It threw me. Was he really feeling me like that?

"Yeah, you're right," he agreed, but his tone was dripping with sarcasm and his face was expressionless, giving an edge to his words that made me feel bad all over again.

"I didn't mean it like that, I just—"

"Sir, can I get you another drink?" Mike asked the man in front of him, obviously ignoring me.

Pursing my lips and frowning, I turned away to focus on a group of women who'd walked up to my side of the bar, although I was painfully aware that their eyes were on Mike. The stabbing feeling in my gut reminded me of my lie. I *was* jealous, though I hated to admit it. But was it really that obvious?

Teema

"*W*here you goin' dressed like a thot?"

Rolling my eyes, I kept my back to Kane but continued to put my earrings on as if he wasn't there staring so hard at me that I could feel it through my clothes.

"I'm going out with Cyndy and Miyani to celebrate our engagement."

"Shit, if that's how you dress to celebrate a nigga cuffin' yo' ass, how you was dressin' before?"

I rolled my eyes once more before turning around to face Kane with my hands on my hips.

"There is nothing wrong with this dress. It goes to my knees!" I huffed.

"Yeah but I can tell you ain't wearing no draws," he countered back, licking his lips as if he already had the image of my naked ass roaming through his mind.

"I am!"

Before I could move away from his grasp, Kane reached out, held me firmly and pulled the snug sweater dress up and over my hips.

"Nigga! That rubberband shit you got on don't count as draws!"

I almost choked laughing at how crazy he was acting. Not only did my dress go down to my knees, but I'd paired it with knee-high boots. I was fully covered. Yes, the dress was snug but I wasn't about to act like I didn't have a nice body and wear a whole damn sheet to the club. Kane was tripping, and I was just about to let him know that when he stopped me by pulling me into his arms and scooping me into a tight bear hug.

"I'm just kidding, love. You look good as hell though, but that big ass ring on your finger better let them niggas know," he finished, pressing his lips against mine as he squeezed my ass hard.

"Well, even if the ring don't, I sure will," I assured him with certainty. "Ain't nobody gettin' any of this but you."

"That type of shit you sayin' might save a few lives," he added without a crack of a smile.

I didn't know whether mine was one of the lives threatened if I ever tried to cheat on Kane, but I knew I'd never find out. My heart belonged to him and if I was being real with myself, it always had. And even if that wasn't the case, I was smart enough to know not to test him. I'd seen all the many sides of Kane, and I didn't want to ever again come in contact with the killer in him.

After kissing Kenya on her cheek while she fought sleep in her bed, I texted Cyndy and Miyani to tell them that I was on my way. Kane had bought me an engagement gift, a brand new fully-loaded Audi, so I was the designated driver, but I didn't mind. I was more than ready to whip and roll my brand new car around town.

***

Well, I was *supposed* to be the designated driver, but thanks to Sidney's ass—who I didn't even know worked at the club—I was drunk as hell. She gifted me with two free drinks, and although they both tasted so good you couldn't even tell liquor was in them, it was obvious they were loaded down.

"How you know her? She nice as hell with the drinks," Cyndy asked, smacking loudly on hers. To be honest, it didn't matter what Sidney had put in her drink; Cyndy was a damn lush and after all the drinks she'd had, it was doubtful that she could even taste her current drink.

"Who, Sid? We all grew up together! I didn't talk to her much… she always been on the boyish side, even though we all knew her and Yolo had a thing goin' on."

"Yolo?" Miyani squinted her eyes at me. "The fine ass brother Kane got that got all the golds?"

"No, girl, that's Outlaw," I clarified, rolling my eyes. "And he ain't even got them golds no more. Took them out for his girlfriend."

I watched as Miyani's nose curled up. "Girlfriend?" she asked and I nodded my head while taking a sip of my drink. "Well, what kind of girlfriend can she be if she's trying to change a nigga?"

For some reason, I felt the need to stand up for Janelle. She wasn't my friend and I didn't know her like that, but I liked her and I liked the type of person Outlaw was becoming with her in the picture. Miyani had taken more than a few men from their girlfriends in the past, and I didn't want her setting her sights on Outlaw. Janelle was good for him and I didn't want her messing up a good thing.

"She's the kind that is worth a nigga changing into a grown man for, apparently. She didn't make him change. He wanted to."

There was a beat of silence and I noticed Cyndy and Miyani exchanging glances.

"Damn, you already taking the sis-in-law's side, huh?" Cyndy cut her eyes at me but I didn't even respond. Definitely didn't mention that Outlaw and Janelle were split for the moment.

I loved Miyani like a sister but I also loved Outlaw like a brother, and she was not the one for him. At some point, Outlaw was going to have to get out the streets and he needed a woman who would stand by his side and allow him the peace of mind to do that. Janelle was the perfect one for that. She and Outlaw were the perfect match. Miyani would have his ass robbing shit until he was old and grey just to support her shoe habit.

We all vibed for a while in the club, listening to the music and swaying in our seats to the beat. Miyani hit the dancefloor a few times, but Cyndy seemed so into her phone, she could barely enjoy herself.

"Who is the new bugaboo that can't stop hittin' you up so you can have a good time?" I asked her, finally. I'd been waiting for her to tell me but when she didn't, I figured I was going to have to ask.

Cyndy raised her head and looked at me like she was confused. After running my words through her mind a few times, it clicked what I was asking.

"Oh! No, girl, this ain't no man. This just some chick I know… bothering me."

"Well, tell that hoe we tryna turn up!" I laughed and raised my glass. Cyndy joined in but only half-heartedly. Something was up, but I wasn't going to press her to share it with me. If she wanted to ruin her night texting some heffa who was annoying her ass, that was on her.

"When is the last time you spoke to your mama?" Cyndy asked out the blue and nearly sobered me right up. The hell was she bringing her up for?

"What?! You mean the bitch I two-pieced after finding out that she was stealing my money? The one who is the reason for my baby and I almost bein' put out on the street?" I snapped, and Cyndy averted her gaze. "That was the last time I spoke with her. She kept trying to call me once my phone got turned on but I blocked her number and stopped answering numbers I don't know."

"But don't you care how she's doing?"

My frown deepened. What the hell was Cyndy's deal right now?

"Why should I? She didn't give a damn about how I was doing or how Kenya would be doing when she stole all my money and almost got me tossed on the street!"

Cyndy's face straightened and she pressed her lips firmly together, but dropped the subject. I was grateful for that. This was my celebration and the last thing I wanted was to be reminded of my fucked up past when I should be celebrating my promising future. I spent so much time hating Kane for the things he did, but he'd changed my life for the better now, in ways that I never thought possible. Nothing or no one could bring me down... or so I thought.

Cyndy was still peculiarly quiet when it was time to go, but I couldn't spend my time begging a grown woman to open up her mouth and tell me what was going on. Whatever she had on her mind would eventually be brought to the surface. That was my thought process, anyways. And boy, was I right…

"This spot is live! How you found out about this spot, Cyn?" Miyani asked, still huffing and puffing from showing out on the dancefloor.

"Huh?" was Cyndy's response and Miyani rolled her eyes. We'd both had enough of her being distant.

"Anyways, Teeeemuhhh," Miyani dramatized my name to make a point of ignoring Cyndy. "I had a good time and I hope you did, too. I even got the owner's number."

She flashed a smile at a man standing across from us. I assumed he was the owner she was referring to. If so, he wasn't anybody to brag about. He was much too flashy for me; the type of man who wore every damn chain and piece of jewelry he'd ever purchased in order to prove a point to women who only cared about his pockets. I scrutinized the man further and then cut my eyes at Miyani. She was so obvious with her intentions. The man was short and unattractive. He had a smile like the Cheshire cat and was dressed like a spoiled and entitled toddler in clothes much too big for him. He wasn't her type, but she was going to bleed that little man dry.

"Good luck with your lil' leprechaun man," I replied. She sucked her teeth and then rolled her eyes.

"His name is Kyle."

I rolled my eyes and looked over to Cyndy who wasn't even paying attention. Her face was etched with worry and her mouth was moving, even though no words were coming out, as she continued glancing at the door. Something was off with her and I had to ask.

"Cyn, what is your problem?" I placed my hand on my hips and cornered her so she couldn't help but answer me.

"Teema, listen…" she started. "You know that you're my best friend and I would never do anything that—"

Before she could finish her sentence, I felt a tug on my arm and turned around, locking eyes with Sidney.

"Hey Teema, can you do me a favor and not tell Kane or his brothers that you saw me here?" She bit down on her bottom lip and began to play with her fingers.

"I don't want Yolo to know where I work. We…um…" She cleared her throat and brought strength into her tone. "We aren't together anymore."

My first thought was to ask her what happened, but I stopped when I recognized the expression on her face as the same one I had when I fixed my mind on leaving Kane. Yolo had royally fucked up in Sidney's eyes and although she was hurting, it was obvious she was determined to move on. I knew how that was because I'd been there. And the last thing I wanted was people in my business.

"I won't tell. I promise," I assured her with a nod. "But if you need anyone to talk to, call me." She gave me a nod with her eyes planted towards the floor, and I took off behind Miyani who was already heading to the exit.

The moment we stepped outside, I was reminded about what

Cyndy had started to say before Sidney interrupted us but by then, it was too late.

"Teeeeeemuhhhhhh!"

Just the sound of her voice hardened my heart and I gritted my teeth together. Turning sharply towards the voice, I cringed when my eyes fell on her face. She looked terrible. Hideous even. Her skin was ashen grey in color, like a filter lay over her chocolate skin tone. Her torn and severely stained clothes were much too big for her and hung loosely over her frail, pencil-thin body. Shit, just to be totally honest, looking at her ass scared me. And then, even though I knew my next reaction should have been to be concerned, I was *embarrassed.*

"Mama… what are you doin' here? How did you find me?"

Her eyes flashed to my side and I felt Cyndy tense up. That was all I needed. I turned sharply towards her, but she was already looking at me with panic-stricken, apologetic eyes.

"Teema, I'm sorry, but she seemed so desperate when she reached out to me. I knew if you saw her, you'd understand how much she needed you!"

My head jerked back and I frowned into Cyndy's eyes. "Needed me? Have you forgotten what this bitch did to me? To my daughter?"

"But it worked out for the best, Tee," Miyani interjected, obviously on some peacemaker shit. "You sucked up your pride, went to Kane and now look! Your life is perfect."

Shaking my head, I put my hand up to stop Miyani from speaking.

"Right, but no thanks to her! She didn't know what would happen to me or to Kenya and she didn't care..."

"But, Teema, she said she's sorry. And she's sick!" Cyndy added with desperation when I started to walk away. "Sh—she's dying, Teema. You may be mad at her, but she's still your mother and she needs you."

Sick?

I glanced at the brand new luxurious car that I was walking towards and then back at my mama who looked absolutely pitiful. Next, I glared into the faces of the few people around the front of the club who were watching everything going down with expressions of disapproval aimed at me. My stubbornness began to waver. Was I wrong in still holding a grudge? After all, what Miyani said was true. If my mama hadn't done the things she did, I would still be by myself, struggling on my own and not engaged to the man I never knew that I always wanted.

"Fine," I huffed and turned full-circle to face my mama. Her eyes lit up with a glimmer of hope and I couldn't help but notice the slight twinge in my heart when I saw it.

Don't get me wrong... I still *loved* her. I just couldn't say I *trusted* her or wanted to even be around her. And I wasn't completely sure that I wanted to take on the responsibility of caring for her either.

"You can stay with me tonight and we'll figure things out in the morning."

It took her all of two seconds to run over and meet me at the car with a big ass toothy grin on her face. The whoosh of wind that arrived with her nearly burned my nose. Not only was she supposedly sick—I wasn't sure yet that Cyndy hadn't only said that to get a reaction from me—but she smelled like she'd been calling a garbage can her primary residence ever since the last time I saw her. She was definitely about to mess up my new car smell.

And on top of all this, there was Kane. He'd just bought a brand new house for his new family to live in. I was certain that he'd never expected my mama to be one of the crew. In fact, he really couldn't stand her because of all the things she did to me when I was younger. And I was positive that he really wanted nothing to do with her now. But if she was in fact dying, I couldn't leave her on her own. How was I supposed to deal with all of this?

Janelle

*M*y mama was one of my favorite people. I've always been a daddy's girl, but when it came to advice, she was the expert. She told me everything I needed to know about men, and whether I initially listened or not, I would always find myself repeating the things she used to say when I found myself in a crazy situation. These days, I was repeating one of her warnings in particular.

"If a man ever changes you for the worse, run far, far away..."

For years she'd been gone, but I could hear the words in her voice as if she'd just said them. Luke had changed so much about me... much of which I felt was for the better. But there was just so much that wasn't. Every plan I had for my life I'd deviated from in order to be with him. I'd distracted myself from my family—my father no longer spoke to me and then there was Carmella. The one sister I was closest with was going through a crazy ordeal and I didn't know a thing about it.

And I didn't even want to think about my career situation. I'd always known, from the time I could even plan a career for myself, what I would do with my life. I always aspired to be Janelle, the #1 attorney in New York City... or at least have some of the status my father had. But here I was... jobless. Luke had purchased me a building to start my own practice, but whom would I learn from? It was too soon.

The facts were in: I wasn't the same person I'd been before Luke and I couldn't say that I was better. I'd made all these sacrifices to be with him, only for him to write me off like I was nothing. I felt alone and forgotten… until I realized that I didn't have to be.

And so I packed my things and headed back home.

"Janelle?"

The look on my father's face when he snatched open the door and saw me standing in front of it with two suitcases at my feet nearly brought tears to my eyes. In the short time since I'd seen him, he'd aged considerably. His once tamed and perfectly cut beard was a tad bit overgrown. His eyes didn't even hold their normal jovial glow. But then when he looked at me, I saw a flicker of the light return and I was overcome with guilt. Was I the reason he was only a shell of himself?

"Daddy, I—I wanna come home," I said, trying to keep the tears in my eyes at bay.

One fell anyways but my daddy reached out and wiped it away quickly with a swipe of his forefinger.

"Well, let's get your things inside," was all he said before grabbing my suitcases. He didn't ask any questions about Luke or even ask me why I was standing in front of him, ready to move back in, when I should have been back in New York.

"I'm glad you're home, Jani." He gave me a genuine smile after he'd gotten all my things in the house and upstairs, back in my old room. I couldn't help but notice the crow's feet at the edges of his eyes. He was getting older. My decisions had aged him.

With a silent nod, I sat down on my bed just as he closed the door. After all that had gone down the last couple of months, I had to admit I was happy to be home.

***

I'd distanced myself from Luke physically but he was still in my dreams. It seemed like every time I closed my eyes, I saw his sexy ass face and would start regretting my decision to cut him off completely and come back home. The dreams were always different but the situation was the same. He was always calling my name and asking me to come back to him. He was begging me not to leave. Even in my dreams, I wasn't strong enough to say no to him while standing in his face.

"Jani!"

My eyes snatched open and I startled awake to see Mixie's face take the place of Luke's. She was just as beautiful as ever—a spitting image of our mama.

"I can't believe you're back home," she enthused, welcoming herself under the covers with me. She laid her head back on my pillow and used her arms to prop her head up.

"I can't believe I am either. Never thought I'd come back home a failure."

Mixie didn't say a word right away because she knew what I meant. And, like our mother, she wasn't the type to lie to make you feel better. If you fucked up, you fucked up and you had to own up to it. She wasn't going to baby me, but it was good because the last thing I needed was babying.

"You made a mistake; we all make them and they suck, but it can be fixed. The good thing about being a Pickney is that Daddy can fix almost all of them." She smiled and laid her head on my shoulder. "And he can definitely fix this one."

So there it was. If Mixie knew what happened to me in New York, so did Daddy. Daddy didn't have to ask any questions because he'd already known a little about my situation at work. And, obviously, if I was coming home, Luke was out of the picture.

"I know Daddy can fix work," I told Mixie, struggling to blink away tears from my eyes. "But… who can teach me how to not love Luke? Who can fix that?"

Her lips curled down on the edges, showing that she sympathized with my hurt. She wrapped her arms around me and hugged me tight.

"No one can fix that and it will take time for you to move on. But you can do it if that's what you feel is best. You're a Pickney, and we were raised to be strong and determined. You can make it without him."

I didn't doubt what Mixie was saying. I knew that with time I could get over Luke the same way I'd gotten over my other loves. But the question was… did I really want to?

Outlaw

"*Y*'all some sad lookin' muthafuckas," Kane said, twisting his neck back and forth between me and Cree. "Sad ass niggas. Never thought I'd see the day that Cree and muthafuckin' Outlaw's asses would be sittin' and lookin' dog-faced over a female."

I ain't say shit, just gave Kane a sideways look because I already knew we were going to exchange some words at this meeting. It was the first time we were all together since the fuck up at the last job. *My* fuck up, to be specific.

"Ain't shit wrong with me, bruh. I'm just chillin'," Cree replied, pulling his already low fitted cap even lower over his eyes. "I got 99 problems but a bitch ain't one."

"You a muthafuckin' lie," Yolo joined in. "I saw yo' ass on Instagram all over Carmella's page, lookin' at old pics and shit."

Yolo started to laugh, but Cree only sat back in his seat and crossed his arms in front of his chest. I curled the edge of my upper lip upwards while crinkling my brows, glancing at him out of the side of my eye. I missed Janelle's ass, but I'd be damned if I do some female shit like lookin' through her old ass pictures. Cree had it bad.

"Doc, yo' ass shouldn't be talkin' shit right now," Cree retorted with ease. "Wasn't yo' ass at Tank's last night beggin' him to ask Faviola to give you Sid's new number?"

Yolo's eyes flashed with anger and shame before they landed on Tank's face.

"Nigga, you told?!"

"It slipped out!" Tank held his hands up in the air. Then he cut his eyes at Cree. "You a snitch!"

Cree shrugged and placed his earbuds in his ears, bobbing his head to the music as Yolo and Tank argued. For once, I wasn't joining in on the joking around before the meeting. I was silent and so was Kane, until he fixed his eyes on me. That's when I knew it was about to start. I tried to bridle my temper and get ready for the 'let's shit on Outlaw for fuckin' up' campaign to begin.

"So let's cut the bullshit and talk about the last job. Outlaw, you wanna start?"

I raised my hands in the air as if in surrendering to the court. "Aye, I'll be the first to admit that I fucked up. Janelle shouldn't have even been there with me. We got rules for a reason, and I got a real example of why we came up with those rules to begin with. I been keeping my distance from Janelle… not just because I'm mad as hell at her for not listening, but also because I'm waiting for the heat to wear off and don't want anybody connecting any dots by seeing us together."

Tank, Yolo and Cree kept their eyes low as they listened, but Kane's stare never left mine.

"You been checkin' the wire?" he inquired, referring to how we picked up on information that was circulating, whether in the streets or among the police.

"Fa' sho. I stay on top of it. Nothing relevant to us has been mentioned."

"I wouldn't take that to mean Pelmington ain't lookin' into it. It was on the national news, and he's dead set on finding something to tag our asses with," he said and I nodded.

"I wouldn't underestimate him either."

A few beats of silence passed between us all before Kane spoke again.

"Well, only thing we can do now is wait… You think we should lay low before the next job?"

Furrowing my brows once I realized Kane was talking to me, I slowly nodded my head.

"I think that makes sense for us to do. We need to make sure there ain't no eyes on us after what happened. There were a lot of things, thanks to me and Janelle, that could lead back to us if anyone is smart enough to put them together. Let's chill for a while."

"I ain't got no issues with that," Tank added in. "That's why I stack my bread. Plus, that last job got me sittin' pretty for a minute."

"Same here," Cree and Yolo said in unison.

We talked a little longer about how we would legitimize the money, getting rid of the gold bricks… business shit. But my mind was still on how Kane had let me off so easily. Once the meeting was done, I made it a point to hang back so I could speak with him privately.

"Spades game on Friday," Kane reminded us all as we began to stand up and make our exit.

"Probably only gon' be us there after all the name-droppin'

Outlaw did at Janelle's work banquet last month," Cree joked. I smiled, thinking about the crazy shit I did and would still do when it came to Janelle.

"Naw, the niggas that really need us can't resist showin' up. They'll be here," I told him with certainty. "Aye, Kane, let me speak to you right quick."

Kane nodded at me but waited until after the others had left to walk over. It was important to me that I squared things off between us. We were brothers as well as business partners, and it wasn't good on either end to have shit unsaid just so it could build up.

"What's up, bruh?"

"You getting' soft on a nigga?" I asked and he shot me a confused look. "Usually, we would've came to blows over that shit that happened with the last job."

He laughed and ran his hand over his beard, but then shook his head.

"Naw, everybody got lessons to learn. The only reason I used to put my foot in yo' ass before was because you never thought the stupid shit you did was wrong. Either that, or yo' ass ain't care. This time, you fixed it as soon as it happened. You corrected it and owned up to it. Ain't really shit left for me to knock ya on ya knees over."

Smirking cockily, I stroked my beard. "I guess a nigga gettin' wiser and shit."

"Don't get the big head, nigga," Kane chuckled. "What you gon' do 'bout ole girl? Y'all over?"

I tossed on my Gucci backpack before answering. Just hearing him ask whether Janelle and I were over, fucked with me. I had to take a minute to get my shit together.

"Naw, that's still bae," I replied, not even caring that I was showing my vulnerability and love. Something a nigga like me never did. "Matter of fact, I'm about to pop up on her now. I think I've punished her long enough."

"I think you're right. She don't seem like the type you wanna play games with," Kane agreed, making me raise my brows. "You end up waitin' too long and another suit wearin' ass nigga be sweatin' ya woman. Gon' 'head and make shit right."

"Let me find out bein' with Teema done softened your ass up, nigga. Got you givin' out Dr. Love advice and shit."

He laughed heartily and I couldn't help joining in with him. It was crazy as hell to think about where we were now versus where we'd always been. The same muthafuckas with the 'fuck bitches, get money' attitude were now sittin' 'round havin' heart-to-heart convos about the chicks we were in love with. Shit was crazy as hell.

"I ain't no Dr. Love, but I ain't gon' say Teema's crazy ass ain't changed a nigga. I guess like Janelle changed you."

I grinned, thinking about what he said. He was right.

***

The sun was high but hidden by the clouds, and there were birds and shit chirping happily outside. Basically, all that sweet ass stuff that makes it a perfect day for a nigga to get his woman back was going on. I walked up the stairway to my building, soaking it all in and running the words I would say to Janelle through my mind. I wasn't the poetic type but hopefully I could convince her to take a nigga back.

"Mr. Murray!" Barry said with a big ass smile on his face. "Where have you been? Haven't seen you in a while."

He held out his hand for dap and I returned it before responding.

"I been around… you ain't seen no niggas walkin' up to my shit, right?" I queried and Barry didn't even flinch at my language. When I first moved in and started speaking to him like any other nigga instead of the white boy he was, his face used to turn tomato red and would get redder and redder as he stammered out a response. He was used to me by now.

"I sure haven't, Mr. Murray," he replied with a reassuring smile.

"Thanks. And stop with that 'Mr. Murray' shit."

"Maybe one day, Mr. Murray," he joked as I walked away.

The entire way to the elevator and while I was waiting on it, women of all races tried to gain my attention but I wasn't interested. For the *first* time in my life, I was able to easily turn down pussy. Maybe for another man the shit was easy… but not for me. It just wasn't in my nature. But Janelle had stepped in and was making me do things I'd never do. I guess she'd changed me for the better.

Stepping into my condo, I instantly knew something was off. And it wasn't because I didn't see any of Janelle's things lying around either. She was always neat, and even after moving into my own condo, she treated my place like she was a guest and always cleaned up behind herself. What got me was the *smell*. It was stuffy inside… like nobody had been in my spot for a minute. That wasn't like Janelle. She was always lighting candles or spraying shit around my place.

"Nell!" I called out, but I already knew there would be no answer.

Dread spread up my spine and settled in my chest right where my heart was. Or where it should have been... would have been, had Janelle been here. But I knew for a fact that she was gone. And not just on a trip to the grocery store either. She was *gone*. I was standing inside of a bedroom, looking in the closet where all her clothes used to be.

Everything was gone.

On the right side sat all of my things... lonely and untouched, just how I'd left them. I searched the bathroom, in all of the cabinets, under the bed... everything that could point to the fact that Janelle once lived here with me, was gone. She'd even cleaned out the fuckin' fridge! She'd cleared everything out that belonged to her and left only a half-finished glass of red wine. After all of the time I spent loving her and changing my life for her, that was all she left me to remember her by. I picked up the glass, held it in my hands for a second—almost expecting that it would make me feel closer to her. When I didn't feel any differently, I placed it back in the refrigerator and closed the door.

Grabbing my phone, I dialed her number, but from the way it rang continuously without going to voicemail, I knew she had my number blocked. She was really in her feelings. She was really trying to shake a nigga, crush me in the worst way.

Less than thirty minutes later, I was in Brooklyn, sitting in my car right in front of her old apartment. She hadn't been there in forever, and she'd long ago told me that she was giving it up since her sister had her own spot, but I thought maybe, just maybe, she'd kept it and I would find her there. I wasn't the kind of nigga who prayed but maybe I could borrow some of my grandma's newfound religion and try it out.

Walking up the steps, I was about to knock on the door when I saw the blinds on the front of the window were pulled up. So instead, I decided to lean over and gaze in. I was met by a pair of eyes staring back at me but they were definitely not Janelle's.

"Nigga, who you?" a deep voice boomed and about a second later, the door snatched open to reveal a big, Black, beefy dude.

He had a deep scowl on his face with his teeth bared, showing off a bottom row gold grill. Then after about two quick seconds, his eyes flashed with recognition and his face fell.

"Shit! Outlaw!"

Before I could say anything in response, a thick red-bone chick squeezed by him out the door and positioned herself next to him. The lust on her face was obvious as she stared, but I barely gave her a look.

"Aye, my bad, man. Someone I knew used to live here," I replied, somewhat distracted as I scratched at my jaw. Where could Janelle have gone?

"Used to?" The guy cut his eyes to the chick next to him who was a couple seconds too late from wiping the lustful look from her face. He caught it and nudged her with his elbow.

"Ouch!" she howled as I turned around to leave. I didn't need to be involved in any of their problems.

I was nearly to the car when I heard the guy bark at her, "Bitch, is you fuckin' with Outlaw?!" He mushed her in the head after he'd asked.

"No!"

If my mind wasn't so fucked up, I would've had to chuckle at the exchange, but I couldn't focus on anything or anyone but Janelle.

"Boy, what you stormin' in my house like that for?"

As soon as my grandma opened the door, I rushed in and headed right into the living room to her house phone. When the dial tone finally hit my eardrums, I pressed in Janelle's number and pushed the phone to my ear as I waited. Across from me was my grandma, posted up on the wall with her arms crossed in front of her chest and her eyes trained on me. She had a knowing look on her face, accompanied by a sly ass smirk, but I ignored it. After a forever of constant ringing, Janelle's voicemail picked up. I closed my eyes and listened to her voice, struggling to keep my emotions in control.

"Heyyyyy, this is Janelle. I'm busy at the moment but I promise if you leave a message, I will check it and I will call you back."

Beep!

"How good is that promise?" I paused, even though I knew I wouldn't get an answer. "Call me back."

I hung up the phone and pulled the brim low on my fitted while keeping my eyes down. I wasn't ready to answer any questions. I wasn't ready to deal with my reality.

"You a'ight, son?"

I took a deep breath and shrugged, putting on that I was much stronger than I really was. In reality, I was one step away from being broken. Janelle was gone and I had no idea how to find her. But then…

almost as quickly as I'd thought I had no idea where she'd go, another thought occurred to me. I knew exactly where she was. I gritted my teeth together as I realized that she was so far away from me, but then I relaxed because I knew she was safe.

"It's all good. Sorry 'bout runnin' up in here like that," I walked over and kissed my grandma on the cheek.

"Okay, well, I love you, Luke," she said and patted me on the shoulder. "Whatever is goin' on, I know you'll be fine."

I didn't believe it. But I wouldn't say that aloud.

"I love you, too. Lock up. I'll be back over here tomorrow."

And every day after that, I thought to myself. *Every day until Janelle picks up that fuckin' phone.*

Sidney

*L*aTrese's haunted eyes stirred my soul. She touched my arm and I shivered from her frigid touch. Tears seemed to stall in my eyes as I stared at her, painfully noticing the markings, Yolo's fingerprints, around her neck. The bruising was so deep and purplish blue against her caramel skin... I had to look away.

"Why didn't you help me, Sidney?" she asked and I jerked my head up, staring her in the face with my eyes wide.

"I... I tried! I swear I tried but..."

Before I could finish my sentence, LaTrese's eyes flashed with anger and she gnashed her teeth together. Her fury instantly became so thick around me that it was suffocating. I began to gasp and struggle to take in each breath. And then, eventually, it was like I couldn't get in air at all, no matter how hard I tried. I squeezed my eyes tightly closed, still fighting for my next breath. Then I opened them and realized why. LaTrese was on me like a deranged killer, manically squeezing my throat like she was trying to make her fate my own.

"P-P-Please!" I sputtered with desperation, urging her with my eyes for mercy.

But she didn't stop. She only squeezed harder.

"You should have helped me, Sidney! You should have helped me!"

"I did! I tried!" I wailed repetitiously.

I woke up in a cold sweat, breathing hard and confused about where I was. It took a minute for me to realize that I was in my bed, in my new room, in my new apartment. Standing up, I walked into the kitchen to pour myself a glass of water.

For the past couple weeks, I'd been having the same nightmare about LaTrese over and over again. The guilt of her death was eating me alive. She didn't deserve to die. She was mentally ill and if I'd kept my mouth closed, she would be alive today.

To see Yolo snap so easily was something unnerving for me. I couldn't cope with it. It was like nothing to him to take a life. One minute he was doing everything in his power to keep her alive and then, in the next, he was taking her life away. Not only did he not care that she was mentally ill and couldn't be held accountable for what she'd done, but he didn't even bother to research on his own to see if what I was saying was true. Would it be that easy for someone to make him turn against me? I'd always overlooked the things I knew he'd done with his brothers, rationalizing that he was the most caring of them all, and that he was pressured to tag along when they committed their crimes. Now I knew he was just as savage as them all.

Knock! Knock! Knock!

Riiiiiing!

"I'm coming!" I yelled at the front door and then checked the clock on the microwave.

11:28.

I'd actually managed to sleep in pretty late.

"Who is it?" When there was no answer, I rolled my eyes. If you could knock on my door, you could at least say who you were when somebody asked.

I peeked out the peephole and felt a shiver run down my spine. It was like seeing a ghost. There was a woman standing at my door. She was attractive, dressed conservatively in a nice navy blue and white dress. Her hair was pulled up in a neat bun and she had simple gold jewelry on, nothing too flashy. But what got me were her eyes. Either I was tripping or they were a mirror image of LaTrese's.

Running my tongue over my lips, I took a deep breath and unlocked the door. When I pulled it open, her eyes rested in mine and I almost slammed the door back in her face. Have you ever looked into the eyes of a dead person? Well, that's what it felt like to me. Although the woman in front of me was very much alive and definitely not LaTrese, LaTrese's eyes had been haunting me every night and now I felt like I was really looking right into them.

"Do I know you?"

"No," the woman answered me. "But you may know my sister, LaTrese." She held up a picture as if I really needed to see it. I only glanced in the direction of the photo, not wanting to settle on her image for too long.

"I do know her. She dated my ex," I replied, making sure to speak of LaTrese in the present tense. I also made sure to refer to Yolo in the past because we were through. But it still hurt to think of him in that way.

"I know," the woman replied and then forced out a tight chuckle, pushing her hand towards me. "I'm sorry. My name is Traci. I'm her sister... like I said." She chuckled nervously. I shook her hand.

"I'm Sid." Pushing my dry lips together, I tried to rid myself of the crazy tense feeling in the pit of my stomach. "How can I help you?"

"Well... LaTrese is missing. I spoke to her friends and they told me that the last they knew, she was staying with you and her ex-boyfriend, Yolo. I haven't been able to locate him—"

"And how did you find me?" I pressed, my anxiety making my mouth dry. My tongue seemed to stick to the roof of my mouth.

"I... um..." She looked slightly embarrassed. "I work at the post office. Searched the system and saw your change of address. I promise I'm not a stalker or anything. I'm just worried about my sister, and I seem to be the only one because our parents—"

"Parents?" I gawked at her.

This was too much. LaTrese had always told Yolo that her parents were dead and when I looked into her past, it was confirmed that her crazy ass mother had murdered her father.

"Yes, our parents... through our adoption," Traci explained. I crossed my arms in front of me and stared at her suspiciously.

"How come I went to high school with LaTrese but never heard of you or these parents? She lived with an aunt while she was here," I countered.

Traci sighed deeply. "Tresey accused my dad of sexually abusing her about a year after we were placed in their home. He wasn't found guilty of anything... it was a lie and there was no evidence of any abuse. But still, they allowed her to live with our biological mom's sister. I refused and stayed with my parents. She hated me for that for a while but once we were older, after I graduated and moved out on my own, we reconnected. We talk on the phone every week but I haven't heard from her in over a month. I'm worried something happened to my sister."

Her eyes teared up and the hurt in her expression tugged at my heart. Mainly because I knew the reality of the situation. Something didn't just happen to her sister; LaTrese was dead. She'd never see her again. I couldn't tell her that but I felt like I owed her some sort of comfort. Even though I couldn't give her the truth, I felt like giving her that would help the both of us and soothe my guilt.

"Would you like to come inside?" I asked her, shifting out the way so she could walk in. "I'll help you as much as I can."

Teema

*T*o understand my feelings about my mother, you'd have to understand my life. To put it simply, she was *not there*. For nearly all of my childhood, she was an addict. Her drug of choice changed often but she always loved whatever it was, more than me.

Initially, it would be men. Early on in my life, she actually tried to be a mother, but when her new flame wanted attention and love, his needs always outweighed mine. Then one day, she found herself caught up with Junk, the neighborhood drug dealer. After that, she was introduced to her next drug: dope. She would get high with Junk all day and night, not caring whether or not I ate or was alive. And when she was high, she was drunk. She and Junk drank like fish. To this day, the smell of certain alcohol sickened me to my stomach and I just couldn't deal with the taste.

But throughout all of the things that happened to me growing up, my love for her never changed. As angry as she made me, there was a connection I had to my mama that I couldn't shake, and when she needed me, I was always there. That's why when she promised me that she was clean and begged to move in with me and Kenya, I agreed, easily giving up my bedroom so that she could be comfortable. But after she stole the rent money and almost got us kicked out on our asses, I thought I was released from her spell. Now I saw I wasn't. I was just as easily manipulated by her as I'd always been.

"How long she stayin', you think?" Kane asked in a tone that made the hairs rise up on my arm. His lips curled up in disgust as he looked up the stairs towards the room I'd allowed her to sleep in.

Of all people, Kane knew the history between my mother and I, almost better than I did. In his mind, she wasn't worth shit and, even though I often agreed, she was still my mama and I felt the need to defend her ain't shit ass.

"I don't know. I'm taking her to the doctor tomorrow... I wanna hear what is going on with her health. But if she's really dying... I can't just put her out on the street, Kane."

He snorted and cut his eyes at me. "Why not? She didn't care if you and Kenya was on the fuckin' street!"

"Don't be like that," I urged him. "She's selfish... we both know that. She only cares about herself. But she's homeless, possibly dying and has nothing. I can't just let her be on her own. Maybe she's changed..."

He snorted again, obviously not believing me, and then lay down in the bed next to me. I watched as he pecked away on his phone before sighing and rolling over. I knew the conversation wasn't over, but he wasn't talking and I didn't want to press him. Especially when I wasn't really positive how I could convince him that my mama had changed.

***

"What's your doctor's name so I can look up the office?"

It was the next day; Kane had managed to squeeze out of the house before anyone was awake, only giving me a simple kiss on the cheek before he made his exit. I woke up a little later, after hearing the sound of someone banging pots in my kitchen and Kenya's loud and shrill screams of pleasure. After washing my face and brushing my teeth, I walked downstairs in my robe and was somewhat pleased to see that breakfast was waiting on me, Kenya was dressed and fed and coffee was brewing in the coffee maker.

My mama looked as lively as ever, dressed to the point that she almost looked like an actual grandmother—the kind I'd always wanted her to be for Kenya. She's made breakfast and was cleaning up after herself. With her urging, I sat down and started on a plate that she placed down in front of me and was now scraping the last bits of the grits and eggs onto my fork.

"Um... Dr. Ochobe," she replied distractedly, as she scrubbed down one of my frying pans. It was from the day before. Although I had no issue with cooking, I wasn't the best when it came to washing dishes.

"Ochobe?" I repeated as I chomped down on a piece of crispy bacon.

"Yeah, he's new. But good."

"Is he available today? I want to make sure I hear from him about everything that you're going through. I can call him and—"

"No... No need for you to do all that. I'll call him and check his availability to see if he can see me." She turned around and a grim expression crossed her face. "I—I just don't like to go there. He's already told me about the cancer and—"

"Cancer?!" I shrieked, making Kenya jump. She started to whine and I jumped up to grab her, rocking her gently in my arms.

"Cancer?" I said more quietly. "Mama... are you really that sick? This is serious. Oh my god..."

My voice trailed off and my eyes filled with tears. All this time I'd been ignoring her calls and trying to erase away the fact that she even existed. She was my mama, but because of the grudge I'd held against her, I'd distanced myself from her instead of being there for her when she needed me most. She was the only family I had, outside of Kane and Kenya. She was the woman who gave me life and I'd left her all alone. I'd die if Kenya ever did me like that.

"Yes." She dropped her head and flicked away a tear. "Stage 4 breast cancer. I'm supposed to start chemo... well, I was supposed to start it some weeks ago, but they said I could get really sick and would need a family member around to help me. I didn't want to start until I was able to contact you. Listen, baby, I know that I've done some despicable things but..."

I shook my head and raised my hand to stop her from continuing. "Don't mention it, because I don't wanna hear it. The past is the past and we just need to both move on. I love you, Mama, and I'm always here for you. I'll always be here for you."

I walked over to her, still holding Kenya in my arms, and hugged her tightly. Kenya, sensing that something was wrong, reached up and wrapped one of her tiny arms around her grandmother as well. Before I knew it, a tear trickled down my cheek and I quickly wiped it away. I felt guilty for how I'd acted the past few months when it came to my mama. Knowing that I could lose her was unraveling me. It was unnerving to lose a parent. I'd already lost one before I could even get to know him as a father. I didn't want to lose another.

"I'm going to go get dressed. I'm sure if we just stop by the doctor's office, he can at least tell me what is going on whether you have an appointment or not. It's the least he can do."

I looked into my mama's face and noticed that she was looking down while she wrung her hands anxiously, her brows knotted tightly on her forehead. She seemed worried, and I figured it had to be because of everything she was going through. It had to be hard to hear that you had stage 4 breast cancer in the first place. But to hear it again and again was even worse.

"Okay, baby. You go ahead and get ready to go. I'll get Kenya together and we will be ready when you come back down."

After walking upstairs, I collapsed on my bed and cried, letting out tears that I didn't even know I'd been holding back. It felt like my soul was aching. I was losing a piece of me and the only thing I could do was hope that things weren't as bad as they seemed. I couldn't lose my mama… definitely not now. It seemed like everything in my life was going well and now God had to hit me where it really hurt. I needed her.

Once my tears subsided, I texted Kane to let him know what was happening.

Me: Mama told me she has cancer. Stage 4. Going to the DR to see her options.

Kane: Word?

Such a Kane response. But he'd never been a man of many words so I couldn't be surprised.

Me: Yes. Word.

Kane: *Damn, that's fucked up.*

Placing the phone down, I realized that Kane wasn't the type of person to speak to when I needed to be comforted. Wiping the tears from my eyes, I stood up and walked into my enormous, walk-in closet to find something to wear. When we first moved in, it was pitiful to see how little of it that I could fill up with my handful of clothes, most of which had been purchased from the sales racks at Walmart. But Kane had it built with a goal in mind to fill it with clothing so expensive that a celebrity would probably look at it with envy. We'd only been in our new home for a few months and he'd made good on his promise already, coordinating with Miyani, who loved to shop, and making sure that she grabbed me all the latest and greatest from any expensive brand she could think of.

But right now, my closest was only a reminder to me of how much my life had changed for the better while my mama's had only gotten worse. I had everything I could ask for and she was about to lose her life if we didn't get good news from her doctor. With a sigh, I pulled a simple Louis Vuitton dress off the hanger to put on for the ride to the doctor. Inwardly, I prayed that I would go there and find out things weren't as bad as it seemed.

"SHIT!"

Stomping my Louboutin-clad heels into the cement as I held Kenya in my arms, I stared at my fully flat tire with anguish. As if this day could get any worse, now I had a flat tire. And, although Kane had plenty of cars that I could use, I knew I needed to deal with my flat first. And there was no telling how long it would take to get someone out to tow my car so I could get the tire changed. I knew I could call Kane and he would take care of it, but with my mama staying with us, I'd placed enough of my problems on his shoulders for the time being. I needed and wanted to handle this one for myself.

"You must have a nail or something in here," my mama said, squatting down so she could take a good look at the tire.

I pressed my palm against my head in frustration. "It was fine yesterday."

"Must be a slow leak."

I groaned and looked at the time on the screen of my cell phone. "Okay, Mama, I'm going to call somebody to handle this and then we can get to your doctor. I'll get this handled."

She stood up and pressed her hands against her thighs, dusting them off. "No need. I'll just have Dr. Herring call you later so you can speak to him."

"Herring? I thought you said his name was Dr. Ochobe?"

Her eyes widened and she shook her head, delivering a pressed chuckle. "Yes, Dr. Ochobe. Sorry, Dr. Herring is another doctor in the same office that I see sometimes. I get them confused."

I didn't say anything, even though something about how she was acting seemed strange to me. Going back to my phone, I began searching for someone to call to deal with my tire.

"And... I—I hate to ask for anything, but I'll probably need a cell phone so I can keep up with my appointments and everything."

Lifting up my head slightly, I looked at my mama, wondering why her tone sounded so off. She seemed distressed, and that was my cue to step in and calm her down. "I'll get you one today as soon as my car is fixed. Just sit in the house and relax, Mama. I don't want you to worry about anything, okay?"

She smiled, her eyes lighting up like tiny chandeliers inside. I felt warm inside, knowing that I was finally in a position where I could put her at ease so simply.

"Okay."

Janelle

"*J*anelle! It's good to see you!"

Raising my eyes, I smiled at Tayesha, my daddy's secretary. For as long as I've known, she'd been working with him, and after my mother died, she even stepped up in a huge way, making meals and taking care of us until our father adjusted to life without her. She was hard on him though, pushing him to step up even when he fought against her. She knew that he was mourning, but she also knew he had four daughters to take care of and had to learn how to do the things that my mama used to do. Not only that, but she taught all of us to step up around the house to help our daddy and make life easier on him. It was a long road, but eventually we all made it through and it was all thanks to Tayesha.

"It's good to see you, too," I replied back, but my words didn't match my tone. I kept my head low, not wanting to meet Tayesha's eyes and show the shame in mine. When I got the job with Pelmington, she'd thrown me a farewell party at our house and all, but now I was back here. And, I knew for a fact that Daddy had told her everything, he always did.

"Janelle, look at me, baby," she beckoned me and I lifted my eyes to meet hers. They were warm and comforting, the same as they'd always been.

"I know you may feel a certain way about things, but that's not how I feel or how anyone else feels." I knew she was speaking about my daddy. "We are just happy to see you back. We missed you... we were worried about you and we're happy you chose to come home."

Tears came to my eyes and she stood up to give me a hug. It was one I didn't even know I needed, but as soon as her arms wrapped around me, I felt immediate comfort and relaxed into her.

"And I also want to tell you this," she started, pulling back to look me in my eyes. "Whatever decisions you make for your life, I support you and I love you."

After speaking with Tayesha, I felt a little better about my first day working in my daddy's office. I'd only been back home for a couple weeks and I already had a job. Being that my daddy had his own shit going for him in Atlanta, it was easy for him to pull a few strings and get me a job in his office, working under him in the same way that I'd worked for Pelmington. I'd always wondered if my daddy felt some kind of way for me choosing his colleague over him. On paper, him and Pelmington were neck and neck and, even though they seemed to be friends, I knew they competed against each other. It probably made Pelmington ecstatic to fire me and to let my daddy know why. Either way, now my daddy had his wish. I was back home and working with him, just as he always wanted me to.

"Having fun yet?"

I looked up from the mountain of paperwork on the desk in front of me and was caught up in my daddy's eyes. He was beaming with pride, his smile damn near to the edges of his eyes.

"Yes, you have some really good cases you're working on," I told him with honesty but a little less excitement than I should have had.

He did have a lot of things that I would have died to get my hands on working with Pelmington. However, the bad side of it was that I didn't feel like I earned my way into working on these things. I'd gotten these cases for being a Pickney... it was the same favoritism that I'd been trying to run away from my entire life.

"I'm glad to hear it. But the work keeps coming in so I have someone here who will help you."

A slight frown crossed my face and I watched him intently as he moved out of the way to let someone pass by him. Through the door slid in about 6 feet and 3 inches of pure *sexy as hell*. It was a marvel that I had managed to not drop my jaw into my lap right after feasting my eyes on him.

"This is Darnell King. He's worked with me for some time, sat first chair on a lot of intense cases. I think he's just the one to help you out with some of the heavy, high-profile cases we have coming in."

Darnell walked over to me with his swag at a maximum high. He was wearing a tailored suit that looked as if he'd been poured into it. It fit his athletic physique perfectly. He was milk chocolate brown with light brown eyes and fine black hair, cut low but not low enough to hide his curls. He had a low-cut goatee that only highlighted his perfectly white teeth. There was no flaw that I could see. He was absolutely perfect... And he was holding his hand out to shake mine. Probably had been doing that for a while now, but I'd been too busy drooling over him. Shit.

"Um... I'm sorry, what did you say?" I stammered, feeling my cheeks get hot. He chuckled a little and I swear it made my entire body get warm.

"I was saying that it's nice to meet you. I've heard a lot about you from Mr. Pickney, and I'm excited about us working together."

I couldn't respond because my tongue and lungs had failed me, so I simply nodded my head and shook his hand. I glanced over at my daddy and could tell from the huge toothy grin on his face that this was every bit of a set up. Obviously, he was just as smart as he'd always been and had sent Darnell in here for more reason than one.

"You two take all the time you need to work on these cases. We need to make some headway on them, and soon. Here is the company card so you all can have lunch on me." He reached out to hand Darnell a black card but Darnell shook his head.

"We won't be needing that, sir. You pay me well so lunch will be on me," he smiled and I couldn't help but cut my eyes to look at him. Just as quickly, I turned away when I felt the fire erupt inside of me.

What the hell was happening to me?

I'd spent the last few weeks depressed over not having Luke in my life, and here I was struggling to remember that he was the one who had my heart.

"I wouldn't expect anything less from you, Darnell. You two have fun and be productive."

And then my daddy left... left me with this *man*. This *gorgeous* man.

"So, should we get started?"

I looked up to find Darnell looking right at me, his juicy lips pulled into a half-smirk. I swallowed hard, positive that I was doing a horrible job at keeping my cool and then nodded my head.

"Yes."

***

A couple weeks had passed after meeting Darnell, and I managed to keep myself in check. It was easy not to fall for a person when you spent most of your time avoiding them. Any excuse I could use to work by myself or split up work so that we weren't alone, I used. I made sure to slip out for lunch unnoticed so that I wouldn't have to be confronted by his soft brown eyes watching my face, as he asked me if I wanted some company during lunch. I came in earlier than everyone else so that I was able to leave early, and I worked hard, not taking any breaks, so that I could spend most of my time in my office alone.

Although putting distance between myself and Darnell kept my lust for him at bay, not seeing or hearing from Luke did nothing to stop myself from wanting to be with him. Missing Luke was a constant in my life, whether I tried to keep my mind off of him or not. He was in my dreams at night and took up so many of my thoughts during the day. It was hard to concentrate on my cases without wondering what he'd been up to and what he was doing. Did he miss me too?

One day I was so weak from missing him that it felt like I wouldn't be able to go on if I didn't hear his voice. I almost made the mistake of calling him until I thought about my voicemail messages. My inbox was full of messages that I knew had to be from Luke because all the calls were coming from a Brooklyn number. After listening to the messages and hearing his voice, I ran into the bathroom and cried so hard that I felt like my heart would come out of my chest.

Even though my voicemail was in fact full, it wasn't because of Luke. His last message to me had come about two weeks before. It was a simple message; short, sweet and to the point.

"I hear you, Nell. I know what you want. I'll give you the space you need."

That message is what almost killed me. There was so much devastation and hurt in his tone. It was like he'd finally given up. He finally sounded like he'd accepted the defeat. I'd defeated Luke 'Outlaw' Murray when it came to matters of the heart. All the fight in him was gone.

This was what I wanted, right? I wanted him to stop calling me... to leave me alone so that I could move on with my life and go back to being the Janelle that I was. The one I was proud to be, who met all of her goals, did what was expected of her and never disappointed the ones around her. So why wasn't I happy about that?

I was sprawled out on my bed, face in the pillow and thoughts exploding in my mind as I contemplated the answer to that question, when I heard a knock at my door.

"Jani? You've got a visitor!"

A visitor?

I lifted my head and turned my eyes to the sound of my daddy's voice coming through the door.

"Who is it?"

He didn't answer and instead walked away, his heavy footsteps announcing his exit. Standing up, I couldn't help the glimmer of hope in my heart that it was Luke coming to me. But I knew it wasn't true. There was no way my daddy would have let that happen and be so nonchalant about it.

I ran to my window and looked out, but I didn't see anyone at the door or their car. Whoever it was had already walked inside. After checking myself in the mirror and still being completely unsatisfied with my appearance, I figured I was a helpless case and just went downstairs anyways. Whoever was downstairs would just have to accept me as I was.

"How the hell you manage to catch all the fine ones?!" Vonia huffed, catching me in the hallway right before walking down the stairs.

"What?" I was genuinely confused.

Vonia placed one hand on her hip and trained her beautiful doe-like eyes at me. "Oh, don't act like you don't know who is downstairs waiting for you." She rolled her eyes at my clueless expression. "Only the best for Daddy's *favorite* daughter."

I frowned as she stomped away and made my way slowly down the stairs, paying close attention to the voices I heard below. The most robust one being my daddy's and the other being...

"Darnell?"

The joyous chatter stopped and both sets of eyes turned to me. My daddy smiled brightly and stood up.

"I guess I'll give you both some time alone," he announced happily before making his exit. But not before giving Darnell his look of approval.

I felt sick to my stomach. I was being set up again! Did it look like I was miserable and needed a man to make me better?

Darnell stood and my eyes raked over to his face as he spoke. "Hey, Janelle. I'm sorry to pop up on you like this but..."

"Yes," I interrupted. "You should be sorry because most people call before coming over to someone's house."

Darnell seemed unshaken by my rudeness and only forced out a pressed chuckle and shifted his weight from foot-to-foot.

"That would work if I had your number. I didn't want to intrude by getting it from your dad but..."

"But you had no issues with looking up my address and coming over here uninvited," I interjected sharply with my hand on my hip.

There was a fire in me that had become part of my character post-Luke. He taught me to make demands about what I wanted and to be my own person. Luke took no shit from anyone and I was now the same way. My daddy and Darnell were not going to bully me into what they wanted.

Darnell forced out yet another chuckle and flicked the bridge of his nose with his thumb before stepping forward, invading my space. I sucked in a sharp breath and fought to regain my composure.

"I didn't come here to see you. I came here because your dad needed some papers from the office and asked me to deliver them."

I wavered a little when I realized everything wasn't actually all about me. Damn, I picked the perfect time to get the big head.

"While I was here," he continued. "I wanted to take a chance and ask you out. I've been wanting to do it for a minute now, but you been dodging my ass like a nigga ain't ya type."

My thoughts froze when he eased into the street talk, seeming to become his natural self all of a sudden. He must have read the shock on my face.

"Oh, you must've thought I was some stuck up prep boy from the suburbs." He laughed. "Naw, listen, I'm born and raised in ATL, zone 6. I worked hard for everything I got but I come from the gutter."

I looked at Darnell with new eyes, feeling like I was seeing him for the first time. The cockiness in his tone reminded me of Luke's arrogance, and I couldn't help being attracted to that side. But he *wasn't* Luke, and that made all the difference.

"That's nice of you to ask me out, but I can't. I'll see you at work on Monday."

Darnell seemed like he wanted to object, but he didn't. He left just as pleasantly as when he came, wishing me a good night and saying bye to my daddy before he left. Standing at the front door, I watched as he drove off down the driveway and out of our gates, until he disappeared out of my sight. Although I felt like I'd just gotten hit on by the man everyone may have wanted, I didn't want him. He had sex appeal and everything anyone could ask for, but he still wasn't enough.

I wanted Luke.

Outlaw

"*D*a fuck you think you doin'?" I barked, looking at Gina from out the side of my eye as she stood on the passenger side of my car with the door wide open. "You know what fuckin' time it is. Get in the back seat."

Huffing out a breath of hot ass air, she rolled her eyes at looked at me. "You can't still be on that bullshit, Outlaw. I saw you driving that other girl around in the front seat."

It was obvious she was talking about Janelle, and it was also obvious that she was jealous as hell about the fact that she was about to get her long neck ass in the back seat while Janelle had been riding shotgun in my whip since day one, but I really didn't care.

"Yeah, but that's wifey. You left the nigga who supposed to treat you like that back at ya crib," I replied with ease, not caring if I was hurting her feelings. "Get your ass in the back or stay home."

She sucked her teeth and rolled her eyes once again, doing that shit chicks did that they thought actually meant something to a nigga. But she got her ass in the back seat all the same.

"If she's wifey, then why you been chillin' with me for the past couple days. Where she been?"

I didn't even try to answer Gina's question because it wasn't her business. And if she was half the lawyer that she thought she was, she could figure it out on her own. Janelle needed space, so I was giving her that. But in the meantime, my dick wasn't feelin' that 'space' shit. It was hard enough curving bitches when I couldn't even get my girl to answer my calls. But when Gina showed up in the club a couple nights back, looking sexy as hell, wearing one of them 'fuck me' dresses, I caved without a shred of resistance. She wasn't nothing new; I'd been with her plenty of times in the past. Plus, Gina knew how to play her position when it came to me. As long as I was giving her the dick, she was good. Every now and then, she would complain about how she wanted more from me and blah, blah, blah, but once I told her that she wasn't getting that, she was still cool with it and she knew how to keep her mouth closed.

"That was some crazy shit you pulled at the Thanksgiving banquet. Ole girl must be somebody real important to you," Gina said out of nowhere after we'd been driving in silence.

I lifted one brow and glared at her. Why the fuck was she so intent on having Janelle as the topic of conversation?

"Yo, don't speak on her. Ain't yo' business, for real for real," I reminded her. Her response was to huff out a breath once again, roll her eyes and stare out the window with attitude.

"I just don't understand why she's so fuckin' special."

Errrrrck!

I smashed the brakes in the middle of the street, bringing the car to a complete stop. I was sick of her shit and sick of her voice. The only reason I hung out with her ass was to keep my mind off of Janelle, but so far, she was obsessed with bringing her up.

"Get out."

"WHAT?!"

I looked through the rearview mirror into Gina's shocked face, not at all surprised about what I found there. Of course she was surprised. She was a lawyer, the upper echelon of women as far as she was concerned, and she was used to dating men on her level who treated her like she was a gift to them. But all her degrees, upbringing and shit didn't mean a thing to me, and I wasn't the type of nigga who was patient enough to put up with a person once I was tired of her ass.

"I said, get out!"

She laughed incredulously, looking out the window at the scene around us. Cars were pulling by us, drivers were mean-mugging my ass as they pulled through, but I didn't give a damn. The car wasn't moving until she got her ass out.

"All this because I asked about your bitch?!"

That was it.

Jumping out of my side of the car, I grabbed at the Gucci belt on my jeans and adjusted my fitted cap on my head before walking over to her side of the car. I grasped the door handle and snatched that bitch open, while she stared at me with a surprised, mortified and embarrassed expression on her face. Her fault. If she'd done the shit on her own, I wouldn't have to make a scene and do it for her. Reaching into the car, I grabbed her roughly by her arm and pulled her out. She tried to fight against me, but I easily overpowered her when her Louboutin heels buckled and she nearly fell to the ground.

"I can't believe this shit, Outlaw! You could at least take me home!"

Without saying a word, I leaned back in the car and grabbed her purse, tossing it at her before slamming my door closed and walking back to the driver's side of the car. It was at that exact moment that Gina seemed to come to her senses.

"I'm sorry, Outlaw! Don't leave me out here in the—"

She tried to run over to the door and grab it open but I was too quick for her. By the time she was able to high-step in her heels over to my car, I was already inside and had locked the door. I'd had enough of her shit, and what she had between her legs wasn't enough to make me change my mind. Thrusting the car into 'drive', I pulled off without giving Gina a second look. I was barely down the street before she started blowing up my phone. I ignored the calls for a bit before it got too much for a nigga's nerves, and I ended up blocking her number.

I wasn't myself without Janelle. Shit made me wonder who the hell I'd been before I met her.

"You look green in the face, nigga. Lemme guess... ol' girl ain't call you back yet?"

"Shut up, nigga," I replied back to Kane, walking into his house. Normally, I would have posted up at Cree's but he was on his way out of town. He was being all top-secret about it, too. Wouldn't tell none of us where he was going. If I'd been on my game, I would have grilled his ass about it, but I didn't because I had my own problems and wasn't in the mood to insert myself into his.

"Aye, I'm just tryin' to be here if you wanna talk and shit," Kane replied with his hands up and a slick ass look on his face. I knew his ass was probably low-key enjoying my misery. He'd always told me that after the shit I put women through, I was certain to get it back full-circle. I guess he was right.

"I don't need nobody to talk to about shit because I'm good." He gave me a look that said he didn't believe it but didn't say anything else.

The front door opened up and in walked Teema, holding Kenya, along with a woman I hadn't seen in a long ass time. In their hands were a shit load of bags. After the conversation I'd had with Teema concerning the woman by her side, I was surprised to even be looking at her. Definitely shocked as hell to see they'd been out shopping together.

"Luke!" Teema yelled and ran over to give me a hug. Kenya reached out to me and I grabbed her up, kissing her on her cheek. She squealed and then started to giggle.

"Aye, I missed yo' lil' ass," I said to Kenya and she only smiled in response.

"What about me?!" Teema's mama yelled out, running over in front of me with her hands on her bony hips. I figured it wouldn't be nice to say exactly what I was thinking, so I only looked from her to Kane and then back to Kenya. Apparently, she didn't take the hint.

"You ain't miss me, Lukey-Luke?"

The fuck?

"Hell, naw!"

Giggling awkwardly, Teema looked at her mama. "Of course he did, Ma. Let's go put your bags in the room. You got a lot of stuff and we need to hang it all up. Let me help you."

Frowning, I eyed Teema and then looked at Kane who shrugged. That bitch was staying *here?* The same one who was the reason that Teema was nearly put out on her ass in the cold New York City streets before? Now she had a room at Teema and Kane's crib? What the fuck had I missed?

"Okay, fine. Lukey-Luke, don't leave before you see me try on all my lil' pretty things," she sang in a sickening voice before dancing her ass down the hall behind Teema.

"Da fuck you got her ugly ass over here for?" I inquired, staring at Kane who only shrugged again. I handed Kenya off to him, too disgusted to even play with her at the moment.

"Teema said she has cancer... stage 4. She wanted her to move in so she can look after her in her final days."

"That bitch ain't in her final days of nothing." I screwed my face up, looking down the hall where they'd disappeared. "In here eye-fuckin' a nigga and shit. Muthafucka ain't dying. Why you lettin' Teema get played like that?"

Kane pressed his lips together before speaking and then finally raised his eyes to look at me. "Man, ain't shit I can tell a woman about her mama when she thinks the chick is dyin'. What I do know is that sooner or later, she'll find out that she's being played."

"Like a fuckin' game of checkers," I added, shaking my head. "That's some bullshit, yo'. You should tell her. I don't like my homie gettin' played like that."

"Listen to me... I know Teema and she got a crazy ass bond with her mama. When she thinks she's in need, ain't nothing anyone can do to get through to her. But she's not dumb and she'll figure it out." Kane exhaled sharply and then changed the subject. "Anyways, what are you goin' to do about Janelle? I know you ain't gon' let her get away that easily."

Taking off my hat, I ran my hand over my ragged locs and sighed deeply. "Man, I don't know. I don't want to push her... I want to give her space to get her head together, but I don't want to force her. I'll end up bein' just like all the other muthafuckas in her life if I do."

"It ain't pushin' if you just showin' her what she already wants and lettin' her know that it's time to make a decision. You know where she is?"

I nodded my head. "Hell yeah. She back with her folks. Ain't take me too long to figure that shit out at all. Not like she had a lot of places to run. And she's so damn predictable. Of course, she'd run right back home to Daddy." I tried to ignore the stab in my chest from acknowledging that she'd ran back to that nigga.

Kane lifted one brow and ran his forefinger along the top of his lip. "You going to go get her?"

"Yeah... and I think it's about that time."

Carmella

I did it. I *finally* fuckin' did it. After what felt like forever and another fifty days, I was done with the drug rehabilitation program that my daddy had placed me in, and I was about to be set free.

"Congratulations, Carmella. I'm so proud of you," my therapist, DeNetta, said to me as she handed me my certificate of completion.

I looked down at it with tears in my eyes, feeling even more proud than the day I'd been handed my high school diploma. I felt like I'd taken back control of my life. When I thought about all the things I'd done to get high and the crazy ass situations I'd placed myself into, all I could feel was shame. When Cree brought me back home and dropped me off at my daddy's doorstep, as he explained the reason I was there to my daddy who looked on with a shocked expression on his face, I thought he was ruining my life. It took a long time for me to realize that he'd actually saved it.

"I appreciate you, DeNetta. But I mean it when I say that I hope to never have to see you again."

She laughed at my words and then pulled me into a tight hug, making me feel all warm and fuzzy inside.

"Even so, if you need me, promise that you'll call."

"I will," I vowed.

And I meant it. I was realistic about my recovery and I knew that

I would still have urges from time-to-time, but I also believed in my own strength and the strength of my circle to keep me from going back to the dark place I'd escaped from. Thinking about my circle made me think about Cree. After all he'd seen and all that he knew about me, I was hoping that he still loved me and that we could make things work between us. But I was trying to be realistic about that as well. The last thing he told me was that he wanted me to get better and would see that I did, but that nothing had changed. We—us together—couldn't be.

"Daddy!" I screeched as soon as I walked into the visitation room and saw him standing right ahead of me with a huge smile on his face. I was about to run over to him when I stopped mid-step, noticing a familiar figure to his side take a stand. My face dropped when I realized that I was looking at Cree.

And might I add... he was mighty, *mighty* fine. Better than I remembered and even better than I'd imagined over the past few months since I'd been in rehab. He was drool-worthy... if ever I'd lost my dignity enough to drool over niggas. I mean, *gotdamn* he was fine.

"I'm proud of you, Carmella," my daddy said, kissing me on my forehead.

I hugged him tightly and felt so at peace in his arms. Just to smell that familiar scent made me feel at home. During the process of recovery, they hadn't allowed me any visitors at all. I couldn't even make a phone call. It was a tough journey but it worked.

"I wanted to see you... to be here when you got your certificate," he told me as he pulled back, still holding me by my upper arms. "But

Cree, here, is going to take you home. He asked if that was okay and I agreed."

My eyes widened in surprised and I looked from him to Cree as he turned to face him.

"I know that your lifestyle isn't ideal but I can't ignore the fact that you saved my daughter's life. You brought her back to me when she was going down the wrong road. I can't ignore your dedication to her recovery and to seeing that she makes the right decisions. Thank you."

He reached out his hand and shook Cree's. All I could do was stare back and forth between them like a little kid watching a miracle take place before my very eyes. Who would've known my daddy would *ever* shake hands with a Murray?

The ride back home was about two hours and I was excited about being alone with Cree during that time. At the same time, I was nervous. I hadn't been around him in months and the last time I'd seen him was on the worst of terms. He had been disgusted with me. For as long as I lived, I felt like I would never forget the expression on his face when he walked up on me when I was about to be raped because I'd been standing out waiting to be served by my dealer. That was probably my worst moment in life.

"I'm proud of you, too," Cree said, breaking our silence once we were on the road back home. He glanced at me and I couldn't bite back the smile on my lips.

"I wasn't sure if you'd stay the entire time... I wanted you to understand how important it was for you to get yourself together, but

I knew you had to understand it for yourself and that I couldn't make you see it. I'm glad you stayed. You look good, Mel."

The tingles in my chest erupted like a volcano and my cheeks got hot. I turned to look out the window and enjoy the scenery a little to distract from the warm fire that was igniting in my belly. Yes, I was still very much in love with Cree. I still wanted him very much.

After licking my lips and swallowing hard, I finally had the courage to ask the question that had been on my mind. Not directly... a bitch didn't have *that* type of courage.

"What about us... I mean, are we—"

"Right now, it's all about you, Mel," Cree replied quickly, cutting me off before I could finish my thought. "Focus on you. It's okay to be selfish right now. You need to be selfish. What we had... just don't think about it right now, okay?"

I glanced at him and noted that his brows were knotted tightly together, like he was frustrated about not being able to say what he wanted to say. I knew what that was all about. I'd been told that it would happen. I was told that people around me would struggle to give me bad news for fear that it would catapult me back into using again. What Cree wanted to say to me was that there was no *us*. But he didn't want to be too direct about it for fear that it would drive me to feel depressed or sad and try to self-medicate. That wasn't the case, but I respected his need to protect my feelings.

"Okay," was my only reply.

Cree turned on the radio and I was grateful for the noise to distract from the awkwardness between us. Still, I couldn't help the thoughts from circulating through my mind. For the first time in my life, Carmella Pickney, Ms. SexyCaramel69 who all the men drooled over on Instagram, was in love with a man who simply had stopped loving me back.

***

"Carm!"

I jumped up and almost screamed until a hand clamped around my mouth, silencing me. In my state of panic, I couldn't even place where I was and started fighting against the hand, noticing that I was not in the place that I'd been for the last couple months: the rehabilitation center.

"Carm! Calm down! Daddy told us not to wake you up but biiiiiitch, you know I had to come up in here."

Vonia?

I stopped fighting enough to open my eyes and realized that I was home in my bed, and it was actually my youngest sister who had her lil' greasy fingers clamped down on my mouth to keep me quiet. I blinked a few more times and saw Janelle and Mixie behind her; each of them sitting on the foot of my bed with solemn looks on their faces.

"Shit, who died?" I asked as soon as Vonia moved her hand away from my mouth. Janelle and Mixie exchanged glances but neither of them spoke right away.

"Girl, nobody. They actin' weird like they always do. Now tell us… where you been? Daddy sent you to live with some nuns for a minute?"

Brows straight up in the air, I looked from Vonia's face back to Mixie and Janelle's, noting that they were avoiding my eyes. It was obvious they knew exactly where I'd been and hadn't told TreVonia a damn thing.

"No, Vonia. I was in a drug rehab program. I needed to get clean from—"

"*Rehab?*" Vonia parroted and I nodded my head. "Damn, I mean... I try a little shit from time-to-time, you think Daddy gon' send me too?"

I rolled my eyes and Janelle and Mixie both collectively sighed. TreVonia always made every damn thing about herself. But this time I didn't mind it. Sparing me the questions about my stint in rehab was just fine with me.

"What time is it?" I asked, turning around to find my clock.

After dropping me off, Cree left but said he would be back in the morning. He told me that he was going to stay a few days but would be in a hotel. I tried not to get excited about the fact that he'd be in my city a little bit longer and that I would see him again, but it was hard. It seemed damn near impossible to turn off love. I was so love sick that when I got home, I didn't even want to eat. My sisters weren't in so I walked straight up to my room and climbed in the bed. Even though I'd meant to only close my eyes for a few hours so that I could get Cree off the brain, here it was the next day and I was just waking up.

"It's almost noon," Janelle informed me.

"Noon?!" I grabbed my phone and unlocked it, wondering if Cree had texted or called me. He hadn't and it was another blow to the gut.

"If you're checking for something from your lil' boo thang, he stopped by earlier today." Vonia smirked. "And he's cute too. You better be glad I love your ass or I would try him."

Ignoring the last part of her sentence, I focused on her initial statement. "What did he come by here for?"

She shrugged. "I don't know. He spoke to Daddy for a little bit and then left."

Pressing my lips together, I tried to hide the devastation in my face about missing out on spending time with Cree before he made his way out again.

"Y'all bitches get out of here," I told my sisters, pushing the covers off my legs. "I've been ignoring my Instagram page for a minute so I need to get my shit together and take some pics."

It seemed like they all rolled their eyes but they couldn't hold back the smiles on their faces. I knew they were happy to see me back and I was just as happy to be back. TreVonia and Mixie left but Janelle hung back a little, just as I knew she would.

"I don't want to ask you a bunch of questions, Carm. But I hope you know that regardless of what I got going on, I'm your big sister and you can talk to me."

For the first time, I looked into Janelle's eyes and realized that she was actually blaming herself for the shit that I'd put myself through.

"Jani, none of this was your fault. I knew I could talk to you but I didn't know that I had a problem," I explained, truthfully. "I didn't feel like I needed help until well after I'd already been in the program. Believe me, you know any time some shit is going on with me, you're the first person I run to. I don't give a fuck what you got going on with Outlaw; I know my ass always comes first."

When I mentioned Outlaw's name, she flinched and I noticed it right off. Her eyes glazed over with the same hurt that I knew I held inside of mine whenever I thought about how I couldn't be with Cree.

"You and Outlaw are no more?" I asked and she shook her head, affirming my statement.

"He did something that I can't forgive," she started, licking her dry lips with her tongue. Her brows crinkled together and I knew she was fighting herself. Fighting the constant war she always fought between what she *should* do and *should* think versus what she actually wanted to do and actually thought.

"He... hurt someone. He did some things I wasn't sure he was capable of and if I let myself accept those things or turn a blind eye to them, I know I'm no better than a common criminal."

It sounded good but I knew it was a load of bullshit.

"Jani, you knew the type of nigga Outlaw was when you fell for him. Shit, the first time you saw him, he was on trial for murder! Don't try to act all self-righteous now when you chose to be with him over the cookie-cutter, perfect guy from your job. Bottom line is, if you're going to stop messing with Outlaw, then that's fine. But be honest with yourself about it. He hasn't changed since the day you met him."

I knew I was giving it to her straight and that it would be hard for her to hear, but it was true and I didn't know how to give it to her any other way.

"You're right," Janelle admitted, and I knew it hurt her ass to her heart to say that I was right, for once, and she was wrong. "But still, I can't be with him. He's not the one for me. Besides…" She looked up into my eyes, a dry ass, fake ass smile on her face. "… I am kinda seeing someone Daddy introduced me to at his job. And I'm inviting him over later on today."

"Yeah okay," was my only reply, as I watched her from the side of my eyes while she made her exit. Pursing my lips and shrugging, I walked into my bathroom to get my hygiene together so I could get dressed and ready to put my fat ass on the 'Gram as my way of apologizing to all of my followers.

I didn't know who Janelle thought she was fooling, but it wasn't me. As much as she wanted me to know that she was someone I could speak to about my problems, she wasn't doing the same when it came to me. Her reasoning for not being with Outlaw was flawed and fake, an excuse that she was using for the time being. But I also knew I didn't have to say a word because the Outlaw I knew would find a way to get back at her ass when he felt the time was right. There was no way he was going to let my sister, who obviously still wanted him, be on her own.

Sidney

"*I* think that I want to go see Yolo today. I don't know much about him but I'm positive that he has some answers about what happened to my sister."

Yawning, I frowned as I held the phone to my ear. Traci hadn't been in town long but she was already showing herself to be even more of a pain in the ass than her sister had been. Every single day she called me at the crack of dawn wanting to either talk about her plans for the day to get closer to what happened with LaTrese, or to discuss her findings from the day before. It constantly put me on edge and I wanted her ass to go home.

LaTrese was dead. I had no idea what Yolo had done with her body but I knew that Traci would never find it. But the last thing I needed her to do was to contact the police and have them poking around and trying to find what happened to her because I knew all roads would lead to me and Yolo. We were the ones she'd been with last.

"Traci, I keep tryin' to tell you... LaTrese probably just don't wanna be bothered with you like that anymore. You said that she was kinda pulling away. Maybe she just needed some space and she'll contact you when she's ready."

"No," she retorted. "I know my sister... even though I spent a long time distant from her, I know that she wouldn't just disappear without saying anything to me. She wasn't that type of person. She wouldn't do that to me."

Rolling my eyes, I tried to ignore the way that Traci spoke about LaTrese like she was an angel, turning a blind eye to all the things she probably knew her sister was capable of.

"But Traci, LaTrese had mental issues so—"

"How do you know that?" she cut in with a stark tone, as if LaTrese's mental history was protected information. "How do you know anything about her medical history?"

"I don't know; it must've came up somehow back in high school."

"Mmhm." Traci didn't seem convinced. "Well, I'm going to go see Yolo today."

"No, I suggest you don't," I responded quickly. "Yolo and I have been dating the past couple months and I assure you he had nothing to do with LaTrese."

"That's not what her friends said when I asked them."

Something about her tone annoyed me and I wanted to slap the shit out of her. Like literally wished I could reach through the phone and tap up her face with my fingertips. It seemed to me that she had spoken to LaTrese's lil' funky friends and was now trying to insinuate that she and Yolo had something going on behind my back. If I didn't need to keep her ass close so I could make sure she wasn't doing anything to get me caught up, I would have cussed her ass out.

"Well, I don't know what LaTrese's friends said, but I know Yolo and he wasn't dealing with her on that level." My phone beeped and I looked at the screen. When I saw Faviola's name, I knew that there had to be some bullshit on the horizon. She never called me this early in the damn morning otherwise.

"Let me call you back, Traci," I said, not waiting for her to respond before I clicked over to the other side. "Yes, Favi?"

"I need you to get your ass over here, Sid. NOW!"

From the sound of Faviola's voice, she'd been crying and that definitely threw me off guard. You see, my bitch *never* cried about nothing. Faviola just wasn't built like that. She was ghetto bred to the core and all her mother had were brothers, so Faviola was basically raised around a group of men who demanded that she be tough. It was some of that toughness that made men intimidated by her because she wasn't as 'feminine' as the next chick. I guess that's why we clicked because I wasn't as feminine as the next either. I was about as hard as they come and it took Yolo to turn me into the semi-girly girl I was now.

"What's goin' on?" I asked her, but I was already up and heading to the bathroom to get myself together.

"I can't say the shit over the phone, but I swear that if I see this nigga, he gon' diiiiiiieeeee!" She wailed through my ear so loudly, I had to pull the phone away. "He gon' die tonight, Sid. I swear! How could this nigga hurt me like this? I promise I wanna kill him!"

Just like I'd figured, something with Tank. And I didn't have to think too far from there to know that it had to be something involving him and another woman. Tank was a good guy, but he was a whore in every sense of the word. The nigga just couldn't keep his dick in his pants. But whatever he was working with must've been some good shit to have Faviola stuck and crying over his dick-friendly ass.

About thirty minutes later, I was sitting inside of Faviola's living room, looking into her puffy eyes as she dabbed at them pitifully. Her hair was no longer platinum blond. She'd traded that color for a burnt orange weave that actually set well against her complexion. She had on some deep, burnt orange lipstick to match her hair, and I couldn't say it looked bad at all. Faviola reminded me of Keyshia Ka'oir. She was the type of chick who could get away with all those crazy ass colors and still look good with it. Meanwhile, I couldn't even wear red-tinted lipgloss without looking out of place.

"I've been hearing rumors that Kane got a bitch pregnant. It's been three months since I found out about losing our baby. The bitch is supposedly three months pregnant! So what the fuck? He decided to grieve for our child by jumping in between her nasty ass legs?"

Faviola lifted the clear, designer glasses from over her eyes and dabbed at her face. She had her intellectual ghetto swag going on today.

"Favi, are you and Kane even in a real relationship or is this a situationship?" I asked her, and she made no effort to answer me. "You remember when I was goin' through shit like this with Yolo when he got with LaTrese? I was basically the side chick, and you used to always tell me how stupid it was to let him treat me like that."

"I'm *not* the side chick," Faviola interjected with her correction. "And what da fuck you takin' his side for?"

I sighed and shook my head. This was a lost cause. She wasn't in the headspace to hear any reasoning.

"I'm on your side, of course. So what you wanna do?"

***

Why in the *hell* did I ask Faviola that bullshit?

Now I was standing in front of the Murray brothers' grandmother's house, watching her ass go the fuck off on Tank. She'd changed into her 'fighting wig' for the occasion, a long blond number that waved back and forth in the air as she snaked her neck at him while spurting out curse word after curse word. Truth was, the shit was funny to look at, and Tank looked like he wanted to crawl in a hole under the ground while his brothers looked on.

Well… not *all* of his brothers. One in particular was speaking to another woman, who was also near their grandmother's house with her own agenda in mind. And this was the one that I couldn't keep my eyes off of.

Imagine rolling up on the Murray brothers so Faviola could confront Tank and being reminded of the bullshit that I was going through.

"Tell me what that bitch's name is!" Faviola was screaming.

Outlaw, Cree, and Kane seemed so used to the bullshit that they were barely paying attention. Outlaw had a blunt sticking out one side of his mouth as he texted on the phone, Cree was staring off into space while sipping from a red cup—most likely some stuff that Yolo had mixed up—and Kane had a big ass chicken wing bone in his mouth, munching happily like he had his blinders on to the drama.

My eyes kept going over to Yolo who was a ways off, on the corner, having a conversation with Traci. They were much too far away for me to hear what was going on or to even see me, but I definitely was picking up all I could from their body language. Traci claimed she wanted to speak to Yolo to inquire about her sister but, from the looks of it, LaTrese was the last thing on her mind. While speaking to Yolo, it was obvious that she was under his spell, winding her hair around one finger as she gazed at him with flirty eyes. Her back was tight and her breasts were pushed up and right at him. She definitely had the 'he can get it' pose on lock.

But what pissed me off was that Yolo was no better! His ass was giving her every reason to believe that she could get it too. He spoke to her with his face close to hers, his body leaning into where she stood and repeatedly touched her arm with the tip of his fingers as he spoke. What the hell were they going over that required all that touching and fondling?

"Favi, you betta leave outta here with dat bullshit 'fore my granny come out here and whoop your Black ass!" Tank warned her, earning my attention. Tank wasn't just sending off an idle threat. Their grandma would *definitely* be out here ready to stick a foot up Faviola's ass if she didn't calm it down. I'd figured she wasn't home.

"Naw, she ain't gotta worry 'bout Grandma whoopin' her ass," Outlaw cut in, finally looking up from his phone as he puffed his blunt. "She a good Christian now. I saw the white Jesus she got in there hanging over the fireplace. He for damn sure ain't tellin' her to whoop nobody ass."

"White Jesus?" Cree said, wrinkling his nose at Outlaw. "Yo, she trippin'. Jesus ain't white."

"Tell her ass that." Outlaw shrugged.

"I don't give a *fuck* 'bout your grandma; you gon' tell me—"

Before Faviola could finish the rest of her sentence, the front door opened and out walked who I knew for a fact did not play. And from the scowl on her face and the wooden broom in her hand, she didn't give a damn who she had hanging up over the fireplace. She was about to whoop some Black ass. She cracked the broom down on the sidewalk before starting to speak, and I couldn't help but cut my eyes over to Yolo and Traci. Now he was running his fingers down the side of her body as he spoke all sweetly in her ear. She was smiling hard like she was already in love, and I swear I wanted to beat her ass. I know, I know... you never attack the woman because she don't owe you nothing; you supposed to go at the man. Well, in this case, I really didn't give a shit about all the small details. I wanted to beat his monkey ass and hers too.

"Little girl, get'cho raggedy ass off my property 'fore I knock this broom upside your head! Tank, I done told you 'bout tellin' these ragamuffin lil' girls where I stay!" Grandma Murray bellowed out, so loud that she'd gotten Yolo and Traci's attention. He said something to her and then ran off to join us. I turned around and focused my attention on everything in front of me, gritting my teeth but trying my hardest to ignore him. The last thing I wanted him to see, after avoiding him for so long, was me sweating him over another woman. LaTrese's sister at that! It was almost like history repeating itself.

I figured that Faviola would take the warning and leave, but I'd underestimated the level of hoodrat in her. When she cut her eyes at

Grandma Murray and started snaking her neck around, I knew this was about to be all bad.

"I ain't 'bout to go nowhere until your grandson—"

"Aw, hell naw," I whispered under my breath and stepped up to grab my friend before she got a broomstick stuffed into her rib cage. "Favi, let's go. We ain't 'bout to do this here."

Her eyes connected with me and she allowed me to pull her back, but she still had some choice words to say.

"Man, fuck you, Tank! Fuck you! I knew you wasn't shit!"

"If I ain't shit and you knew it, why you still fucked with a nigga then?" Tank called out, and I turned to him, giving him a look that said not to egg her on. It was bad enough that he was taking her through bullshit and had her out here acting a whole ass for the entire neighborhood. He didn't have to give her any help with doing it.

"Sid."

Yolo's voice was low but I still heard him, even with all the commotion around us. Even with Faviola and his grandmother tossing insults back and forth. Even with Outlaw laughing at Tank yelling for Faviola to leave before he gave her something for her disrespectful mouth. I still heard him then, and I felt his eyes on me even far before. What did I have to do to rid myself of the love I had for this man? I was a fool in love but I didn't wanna be a fool no more. Didn't that count for *something*?

"Yolo… don't," I told him before he could even get to talking.

I already knew he would say some shit that would be on my

mind all night, thinking that I'd made a mistake by leaving him alone. I didn't want him to influence the decisions I'd made. Hell, his ass had influenced my whole life. Every part of me had been influenced by this man in front of me. Every decision I'd made... even the bad ones that I never wanted to speak on. The one I was too afraid to even tell him about.

"Sid, just let me speak to you for a minute on some real shit—"

"Can't you see I'm busy with this crazy girl right now?" Faviola was nearly uncontrollable now, and I had to use both hands to restrain her from jumping over the fence behind us and getting back to Tank.

"Take yo' crazy ass home, Favi! Ain't nobody over here scared of you. I'mma grown fuckin' ass man and you don't tell me what to do!" Tank was yelling as I drug Faviola back over to my car. Unable to land a punch on Tank, she started looking for something to throw at him. After tossing a tube of lipgloss that she had in her pocket, there was nothing else, so she snatched her wig from off her head and lunged it at him.

"Damn!" Outlaw yelled with a smirk on his face while standing up to get a better look. "Crazy ass bitch done snatched her damn wig off."

"Call me a bitch one mo' fuckin' time!" Favi screamed, clawing at me to let her go. I squeezed her even tighter, trying to figure out how the hell I was going to get her into the car. Yolo read my mind and stepped in front of me to open the door.

"Here you go," he said, quietly.

I looked in his direction but didn't say a word as I stuffed Faviola in the car and shut the door behind her. Lucky for me, she decided to stay in the car and pop her shit through the window. I ran over to the driver's side, fully aware that Yolo's eyes were on me and damn sure happy that he didn't say anything to stop me from leaving. My willpower when it came to him was close to nothing. That's why I'd been avoiding him. When it came to Yolo, I was unable to stick to saying no. At some point, he'd get in my head, and he knew it.

"Sid, you know I like you, but don't bring that ugly ass lil' girl over here again. With her disrespectful ass!"

"Yes, ma'am," I replied to Grandma Murray and then jumped in the driver's seat of my car. Less than a minute later, I was peeling off down the road, half-listening to Faviola as she cursed and fumed about not being able to lay hands on Tank like she wanted to. In my rearview mirror was Yolo, standing right where I'd left him beside the road, watching me with sad, wide eyes as if he couldn't believe that I'd actually left him.

Shit, I couldn't believe it either.

Janelle

"*H*ey Daddy."

I kissed him on his cheek and waltzed by him to the coffee machine to make myself a cup of coffee. Something about talking to Carmella about Luke and having to try to convince her that I was over him and was giving Darnell a chance, made me feel liberated in a way. It was like speaking it helped me put it into the universe and made me feel like I *could* actually get over Luke, that it *was* actually the right thing to do and that I could actually give Darnell a chance.

"You seem very happy this morning," he noted, sipping from his own coffee cup.

"I'm always happy," I replied and tossed him a smile. He nodded and gave me a look that said otherwise but didn't jinx my mood by saying what was on his mind.

"Don't tell Carmella but we're doing something for her today, to celebrate her being home. We won't mention anything concerning why she's been away, but I do want to show her how much we missed her."

"That's perfect!" I exclaimed, mixing the creamer into my coffee. "I planned on inviting Darnell over for dinner or something today. Is it okay if he's my date for the party?"

An awkward expression crossed my daddy's face and even though it was brief, the lawyer in me caught it anyways.

"I'm not sure that today is the best day for that—uh, I mean, I like Darnell and that you're open to hanging out with him but…" His voice trailed off and his brows bunched together. I knew that look because it mirrored the same look I wore when I was struggling with the same thing that he was. There was something he wanted to tell me but he wasn't sure how.

"Daddy, it's okay if Darnell told you what I said to him the other day. It's not your fault how I reacted, and I'm not mad at you for trying to push me to move on. He's a good guy and you're a great judge of character. I know I haven't treated you like that in the past and I'm sorry for that…" I paused, taking a deep breath before I continued on admitting that Luke wasn't the one for me. "… I should've realized you're right because you've always been right."

Running over to where he sat, seemingly stupefied, I kissed him on his cheek again and waltzed out the kitchen before I lost all my nerve and went straight to grab my cell phone to call Darnell. He was sexy so it shouldn't be so hard to spend time with him. I was obviously attracted to him in some way… he definitely had an effect on me. But let's be real… no one could have the same effect on me that Luke did. He was aggressive in all ways, inappropriate in the worst ways, dangerously sexy, and that 'don't give a shit' attitude? Shit, I'm thinking about him again, aren't I?

"Hello?"

"Hey, uh… yeah, I know it's you, Janelle. What's up?" His voice was smooth with a hint of laughter in his tone. It was almost like I could hear his smile through his tone.

"Do you want to come over today? For dinner—I mean, a party. It's for my sister. No big deal. Food... people." I blurted it out like I had diarrhea of the moth. Clamping my hand over my face, I tried to ignore the feeling of my shame. I was such a dork. How could Darnell be attracted to me? How could Luke?

Shaking me head of my thoughts of Luke, I focused back in on my conversation.

"Yeah, I'd like to come over. That's what's up."

"Okay, I'll text you the details. See you then."

I hung up the phone feeling happy to be off of it, but not as excited as I probably should've been. Darnell wasn't a bad guy, but everything in me said he wasn't the one.

***

"He is fine!" TreVonia made sure to announce as Darnell spoke to my daddy across from where we stood watching.

The party was a success so far. Carmella was excited to be the center of attention, as she always was when she was the center of attention. And although she was trying her hardest to act like she wasn't still caught up in love with Cree, it was written all over her face. I couldn't believe that after how my daddy treated Luke, he was so accepting of Cree. I guess it was how they met that made all the difference.

"He's okay," was my reply, and I could feel both TreVonia's and Mixie's eyes on me.

"If you aren't feeling him like that, why did you invite him?" Mixie asked and I shrugged.

I'd tried to make myself be attracted to Darnell but I just didn't see him in that way, and it didn't help that TreVonia had been flirting her ass off ever since he walked in the door. Even now, after hearing Mixie's question and noting my emotionless reply, she was sashaying herself over to where he stood to steal his attention. Really... I didn't give a damn.

I was in the middle of a slightly less than deathly boring conversation with my daddy's co-worker about how much society seemed to be going back to the Jim Crow days, when I saw another car roll up in front of our home from the corner of my eyes. Something made me turn towards it, completely pulling myself from the conversation.

"See, what I'm trying to say is that Trump... Trump ain't shit. He ain't! He would be just as happy if we could only ride in the back of the bus again. Hell, he probably want us under the bus! Let him have his way and we'll all be back fighting just for a seat at the table. You see his lil' supporters getting all bold as it is. I mean... I was standing in line the other day and a white man had the audacity to say to me—"

"Excuse me," I told him, not even waiting for a response.

My heart had nearly stopped in my chest and I felt my eyes cloud over with tears, although I wasn't sure exactly why. The blood in my veins seemed to have gone cold as I looked at the bright red Maserati sitting on gold rims. Flashy, just as I remembered them to be. Other eyes followed mine, all of us waiting to see who it was who would step out of the fancy car. All of their eyes asking the question: which new friend of Attorney Pickney's was driving up in something so ghetto-fabulous as this?

And then he stepped out, his long straight hair braided neatly into a ponytail, wearing a nice pair of slacks that fit him perfectly, along with a long-sleeved button down shirt and a nice vest and suspenders. The sleeves of the shirt were pulled up, showing his tatted up and muscular arms. He looked like the boss of the streets that he was: the perfect bit of gentleman and the perfect bit of thug. How I'd managed to convince myself for all this time that I was better without him, I didn't know. His eyes scanned the yard and I had to make myself close my mouth to stop from drooling as I stared at him, feeling emotions course through me that I'd tried to forget long ago.

And then his eyes finally locked on mine and I froze under his penetrating stare, completely at his mercy, although I'd been training myself for this moment. I knew one day I would see Luke again, and I'd been preparing and training myself not to be weak for him as I'd been since the day I feel in love. But here I was, failing miserably.

"Janelle."

Both my daddy and Luke called my name at the exact moment, and I was struck by a bit of deja vu, reminiscing on the last time I had both men in my presence beckoning me to choose one over the other. If I were forced to choose again, would the result be the same?

"Janelle!" This time only my daddy called out to me. I looked from him back to Luke who was hanging back a little, still staring at me, but hanging back to allow me to speak to my father before coming to him.

Shit... I was just telling myself only hours before that my daddy had been right about Luke and he was bad news. Now I was seeking

Luke's unspoken permission to even give my daddy the time of day. How in the world had I given this man this much power over me.

"Yes, Daddy?" I said, turning to him.

I tried to ignore the fact that it seemed like everyone at Carmella's party was sneaking glances in our direction as they mumbled on in conversation that was barely holding their attention. Their focus was on us. Everyone wanted to know what was going on between the great Attorney Pickney, his favorite daughter and the thug in the Maserati. Even my sisters were staring, not at all trying to be coy about it. Carmella stood up, separating from Cree for the first time since the event started, and began walking over, probably to give me some back up in case I needed any.

"I—I have something I want to tell you," my daddy began and cleared his throat. He dropped his head and looked at his hands, making me nervous simply because he looked nervous.

"I want to apologize for how I tried to control your life," he started and I felt a strange feeling in the pit of my stomach. "You're grown and you've always done everything that was expected and asked of you. You've always made sound decisions... you've never given me any reason to doubt you or to not trust you."

He paused and it was only then that I realized I had tears in my eyes, and also that I was surrounded by my sisters who had formed a semi-circle behind my back. By that time, the other guests had stopped pretending not to pay attention and were full on staring like we were the main event.

"I should have never put you in a position to have to choose between who you picked to love and me as your father. Because the bottom line is, I should always be there for you regardless. And I am always there for you regardless." He looked over at Carmella. "I was able to meet Cree and... he's a stand up man. He took care of my daughter when I couldn't be there myself because I was punishing her for her own decisions. And I realized from there that I was acting in haste at passing judgment on those I don't even know. As an attorney and as a Black man, I should be the first to know that there is more to a person than their appearance. And so..." This time he turned towards Luke and extended his hand, beckoning for him to walk forward. My knees almost buckled under my weight.

"So I asked Cree to invite Luke to attend this party. I know you have your own reasons for coming back home, but I don't want any of those reasons to be because of me. If you choose not to be with him, I want it to be because you chose it. I've had a long conversation with Luke, and he cares for you in the way that I could only wish for a man to love my oldest daughter. I'm done forcing you to live your life a certain way because it benefits me. From now on, you make your own decisions and I'll stand by you."

I kept my eyes low for a minute, trying to get myself together because I knew that I was only a few seconds away from breaking down into tears. For someone who barely cried when I was little, I was always crying now!

My daddy walked away and pulled my sisters away with him, leaving Luke and I alone. I felt about as nervous as I did the very first time he looked at me back in the courtroom. And I was just that terrified as well. I didn't know what to say to him... had no idea what he would say either. The last time I saw him, he seemed to be disgusted with me for being at the wrong place at the wrong time. And then, there were the phone calls that put my emotions in an uproar. The many messages begging for me to come back to him.

But did I really want to come back? I'd had an up-close look at the things that Luke was capable of. Did I really want that to be part of my reality again? And then there was the call that I'd heard between Pelmington and my daddy. I knew that my daddy had handled it already, but did I really want to keep putting him in positions where he had to alter his character in order to protect me?

"Hey," was all Luke said and I nearly turned to mush inside.

Keep your cool, Janelle! Don't let this nigga control you... with his fine ass.

"Hey," I replied back.

Luke extended his hand and I froze, looking down at it as if his touch would crumble the final bit of my resolve and pull me back to his side. I looked back up to him and noted the cocky smirk on his face. He knew the effect he had on me and he knew exactly what he was doing. He was fully aware of my thoughts, of that I was sure. He knew that I was trying my hardest to not be sucked into the sex appeal he'd perfected over the years.

The same sex appeal that made women scream out they loved him in the courtroom where he was being tried for murder, and the same sex appeal that made women perfectly fine with letting him finger them on the train in broad daylight. But no, I wouldn't fall victim to that same sex appeal. I loved him but I had morals and integrity, and I had to hold on to the person that I was, even in his presence.

"I just want to walk with you for a minute... so we can talk. That's all," he explained with his hand still extended between us.

Something about seeing the man I love want to embrace me made it impossible for me to reject him. Especially when every part of my body was calling out for him. I grabbed his hand and definitely did not miss the satisfied look on his face. He was feeling himself over the small victory.

"How you been?"

The small talk was okay, but I knew that it wasn't anything close to what he really wanted to ask me. Still, I wasn't sure I was ready for what he really wanted to ask. Either way, I knew it would come soon. Luke wasn't the type to not be direct.

"Good..."

"You been entertaining any of these goofy lookin' niggas out here?"

There was the directness I was waiting for. My head jerked up and I nearly melted with shame when I saw Luke looking at Darnell who was standing a little way from us. He only glanced at us because, thankfully, his attention was mainly on TreVonia. It seemed that even though he'd come to hang out with the oldest Pickney girl, he was caught up with the youngest. Judging from the look on her face, she was just as caught up with him. I had to admit that they looked good together.

"I'm sure I haven't been doing anything more than whatever

you've been doing with whoever back home," I replied, smartly. Luke must've forgotten he was talking to a lawyer. A funny expression flashed across his face.

"Touché," he responded and my chest burned. It hurt me to think what he may have done with another woman while I was here suffering from not being around him.

You can't be mad at him when you left him, Janelle.

Even though the rational side of me knew that was true, I still was pissed off.

"So you couldn't leave the birds alone, huh?"

Luke looked at me, a comical look on his face like he was about to burst out in laughter.

"Birds? You don't even talk like that, Nell," he replied like that was the point. "And anyways, I wanted to give you some time. I knew you was having a little fit like you always do and taking things to the extreme. I didn't want to push you so... I did what I had to in the meantime."

I turned to him and crossed my arms in front of my chest.

"And what if I did what I had to in the meantime, too?" His face went deadly serious and cold. Like, I literally felt a shiver down my spine and instantly regretted trying him.

"Don't get fucked up out here on yo' people's lawn, Nell."

What?! You see how men are? They can do whatever they want and it's supposed to be no big deal, but we even think about it and they start issuing out death threats. What part of the game is that?

"Oh, you're going to do me like you did the lady from the bank?" I whispered harshly and I saw his face change, growing even colder than it had been before.

"Don't bring that shit up ever again. I know you ain't from the streets, but you're going to learn the rules of the game. You ain't see shit so ain't shit to discuss. Got it?"

I couldn't believe he was here, on *my* property talking to me this way.

"No, I don't 'got it'!" I retorted, snatching away from him when he tried to grab my hand. "And you need to leave."

"If I leave, you're leaving with me."

"No the hell I'm not!"

We sat there for what felt like an infinite moment of time, staring each other down. Both of us too stubborn to accept defeat, but neither of us really wanting to be rid of the other. Finally, Luke sighed and his shoulders dropped. It almost made me smile to see the headstrong, arrogant and unyielding Luke Murray seem to be defeated by a woman almost puny compared to his size.

"What the fuck you want from me, maaaaan?" He groaned out his words like he couldn't even believe he was saying them. And I was satisfied to hear them but had no idea how to respond. After pausing for some time, I finally came up with it. I knew exactly what I wanted from him.

"I want some time. I want to take things slow." He lifted one brow and gazed at me from under his thick lashes.

"Slow? Nigga, we already been fuckin'!"

I tried to ignore his brash response. "I want to start over and get to know you. We rushed and a lot of things got thrown by the wayside in the process. I want to know you... everything about you. If you expect me to be by your side, regardless to what it is you're doing, that means that I could be held responsible. That also means I need to know."

His eyes weighed my words and I watched as he ran his tongue along his teeth pensively.

"Everything?"

"Everything," I affirmed.

"You sure you can handle all that?" He smirked and my heart clenched tight.

I nodded. "I'm sure."

"Deal," he said and I held out my hand to seal the deal. "Naw, I'mma need a kiss."

He was teasing me, trying to make me smile, and it worked. Still, I shook my head at him.

"I said I wanna take things slow, Luke."

His eyes bulged.

"Fuck! How slow we gotta take it?!" I didn't reply. Wasn't sure he really wanted me to. It wouldn't make anything better. He ran his hand over the front of his face and let out a heavy exhale.

"I'm goin' to get a spot here in the city. If you wanna take this shit back to how we started, like you ain't never sat that pretty ass on the tip of my tongue—" I nearly died. "—then we can do that."

Visibly shaken from his comment, I simply nodded my head and turned away from him to continue our walk around the property. Luke walked alongside me, not even trying to grab my hand, but he was obviously the winner in this situation, judging from the smirk on his face.

He knew exactly what his words did to me. He knew exactly what he did to me. And he used it all to his advantage.

Teema

"*M*ama, can you watch Kenya for a couple hours tonight? Kane and I want to catch a movie."

I walked up on my mama, who was laying on the couch laughing at an episode on Family Feud. As soon as I came into the living room and got the last word of my question out of my mouth, her fit of laughter turned into a fit of coughs. I ran to the kitchen to pour her a glass of water. She grabbed it from my hands and swallowed it all down before lying back on the couch, holding her chest and wheezing.

"If you need me to watch her, baby, you know I can. I just—"

Before she could even finish her sentence, she was up again with her hand pressed over her mouth and taking off down the hall to the bathroom. She slammed the door behind her and then the most disgusting retching followed. Yuck!

"What you got that stank ass look on your face for?" Kane asked as he walked down the stairs holding Kenya in his arms. I swear that little girl barely had to use her own feet when he was around.

"I asked Mama if she could watch Kenya for us but she's too sick. I can't leave Kenya with her like this." I gestured towards the bathroom where the sound was still coming from. Kane seemed pretty much unbothered and just gave me a blank stare.

"You sure? I was down here about thirty minutes ago and she

116

looked healthy as a muthafucka while she was watching TV and shit."

I rolled my eyes, noting from his tone that he still wasn't over the fact that he wanted my mama's ass out of the house. I'd told him about her having cancer and he was damn near emotionless about it. I wasn't stupid and I knew my man. Kane didn't believe that my mama was sick and he didn't want her to be under our roof any longer, it was obvious. I couldn't explain to him how I was feeling because I knew he wouldn't get it. He never had issues with his parents and they never needed his help with anything. The way I was brought up was so different from the way he was brought up. My mama always needed me. Growing up, it was only the two of us. I knew that she had made some mistakes, but in the end, I was all she had, and I knew I had to be there for her whenever she needed me.

"I don't expect you to understand, Kane. And it's okay because it's really not your business. She's my mama which means she's family, whether you like it or not."

He gave me a look like he wanted to fight me on the subject, but then just threw up one of his hands as he cradled Kenya in his arms with the other. I looked down at her. She was an exact replica of her father, something that I absolutely hated when Kane and I weren't together.

"What would you think and how would you feel if you were sick and needed Kenya but she left you to fend for yourself? How would you feel as a parent?"

Kane's eyes narrowed into slits and it was at that moment that I wondered if I'd taken it too far. Even still, I stood my ground because I felt like I was right. And if I struck a nerve, then that just meant that I was definitely right.

"First of all, I would never put Kenya in a fucked up position to where she'd have to take care of my ass. I'm not no half-assed parent that wouldn't be able to pay my own damn bills. And you act like ya mama old as shit… she only in her fuckin' forties but never had a damn job. Don't forget this the same lady who had you and my daughter knocking on my door in the middle of the night with no place to go. She's not a parent. It's not the same."

I tensed up and felt the fire of my fury rising up through my bones.

"How could you say that?!"

Placing Kenya down, he looked me square in my eyes to let me know that he meant every word that he was about to say and wasn't expecting much talk back once all was said and done.

"I can say that because every muthafuckin' time she pulls this stupid shit on you and you fall for it, I'm the one helpin' you out of it. I've been draggin' your ass out of fucked up situations with your moms since the day we met, love. Ain't shit changed."

With tears in my eyes, I turned around and ran up the stairs, straight into our bedroom and slammed the door closed behind me. With all the dramatics that I could muster, I flung myself on the bed and cried into my pillow, pissed off at Kane for talking to me like that. We were engaged to be married… how could he make me feel like I was nothing but a charity case for him since the day he met me? If I was an idiot who always needed to be bailed out of stupid shit, why the hell was he marrying me then?

"Fuck him and that stupid date," I grumbled under my breath and continued sobbing into the pillow until I'd cried myself to sleep.

I woke up less than an hour later to my cell phone blaring in my ear. My first thought was that it was Kane calling to apologize, but that thought quickly disappeared from my mind. Kane never apologized for shit. He was slow to speak and quick to listen for that very reason. He didn't like to apologize so he was extremely careful with everything that he said. And you already know that he *always* thought his ass was right.

Peeking at the phone, I saw it was Cyndy. Before I could decide whether or not to answer it, the call ended and the choice was made for me. I hadn't talked to her since the incident at the club. A few seconds later, a text came through. I knew who it was from before I'd even gotten a chance to read it.

Meet me at the Starbucks by your house... please. I'm already there. I just want to talk.

I sighed and rolled my eyes after reading her message. No matter how mad I was at Cyndy, she was my best friend and I couldn't leave her hanging. My house wasn't anywhere near hers so if she'd drove all the way to my side, it was because she was desperate about seeing me.

See you in a few, I replied and pulled my ass up from the bed to get myself together.

***

"Hi Cyndy," I greeted Cyndy as soon as I sat down at her table.

My tone was a little rougher than I'd planned for it to be mainly because I was agitated. My mama refused to watch Kenya for me even to go to Starbucks for a few minutes, saying that she didn't feel good enough to look after her, which meant that I had to do something I didn't want to do and ask Kane's ass for a favor. I hated asking a nigga for shit when I was mad.

"Tee, why haven't you been answerin' my calls? Are you still mad at me?"

Twisting my lips to the side, I paused for a few seconds before answering. Cyndy knew damn well why I had been ignoring her calls. Although I was grateful that she'd intervened so that I could help my mama when she needed me most, I didn't appreciate the way that she did that shit. As my best friend, I didn't understand why she couldn't take me to the side and have a conversation with me about what was happening, rather than letting me be embarrassed to death on my special day.

"Cyn, you already know why I'm pissed at you and I know Miyani has told you. You were dead wrong with how you handled that situation. Me and you been cool since they day we met… you know I don't like causing a scene and I damn sure don't like everybody in my business."

Cyndy was quiet for what felt like a long while. We never really argued about anything so this was new for us. To be honest, I was probably just as ready as she was for it to be over.

"I know and I'm sorry," she said finally.

"I know you are and I forgive you," was my reply.

After that, we stepped right into small talk. She filled me in on her love life. I was shocked to hear that she was still dating Javier, the guy she'd met on our girls' trip to Cabo. It wasn't like Cyndy to mess with the same man for too long so he must've been someone special.

"How is the engaged life?" She eventually asked the question that I knew was coming. The last person I wanted to speak about right now was Kane.

"Girl, it's a'ight, I guess," I replied, putting extra emphasis on the 'guess' and pairing it with a stank ass look to match the stank ass way I felt about love at the moment.

"You guess?" Cyndy's brows perched upwards on her forehead as she peered at me, knowing damn well that I couldn't wait to explain further. Miyani and I were cool, but she was always too into her own shit to listen to mine. Cyndy was the one I vented to and being mad at her had made venting hard to do.

"Girl, Kane giving me shit about my mama bein' around," I started, rolling my eyes before I told her the whole story of what had gone down before I drove over to meet her. By the time I was done, Cyndy had sat back in her chair and was giving me a look that I couldn't quite explain, but I could tell that she wasn't completely on my side.

"What?" I asked after waiting for her to respond. She needed to tell me I was right for going off on Kane… or something like that. Shit, isn't that what best friends were supposed to do?

"I'm sorry, Tee. I'm goin' to have to side with Kane on this one," she replied, shocking the hell out of me.

"How you gon' side with his ass and you the one who told me to take my mama in and watch after her?"

"I told you that you needed to talk to her... to hear her out," Cyndy clarified. "She'd been trying to contact you and I know how you can be when you feel like you're done with someone. You cut them off completely. I thought, being that she is your mother, you needed to hear what was going on with her but... I still think you should be wise about how much you put yourself out there for her. Especially considering your past relationship."

I bit down on the corner of my mouth and watched Cyndy's face, reading her like the open book she was. There was a lot she was saying, but I also knew there was a bunch she wasn't saying.

"What else do you know, Cyn?" My eyes pierced hers, daring her to lie to me. If she really wanted me to cut her off completely, then she could continue to keep the secret that I knew she was holding.

"Well..." she began and cut her eyes away from me, looking everywhere but in my face. "I saw your mama the other day... back in your old neighborhood. She wasn't doing nothing crazy, but I did notice that she was hanging around some people who didn't look like they were up to any good. Just—just watch her and be smart about the shit that is going down in your house. Okay?"

I nodded my head. "Okay."

After about thirty minutes of catching up with Cyndy, I was on my way back home, still thinking on what she'd said about seeing my mama back in our old neighborhood. That was news to me because we now lived nowhere close to where she and I had before. Every time she left the house, she said she was going to get chemo. When did she have time to go anywhere else to hang out with old friends? And where did she find the energy? Wasn't chemo supposed to drain you?

Something just didn't seem right but I didn't want to think the worst. I loved my mama and, no matter our past, I felt my life would be complete with her in it. A girl needed her mother, but I was starting to think that the idea of the mother I wanted—the dream I had in my mind—was not the one that I had, and I needed to realize that.

Turning the corner to my house, I pushed the thoughts of my mama away and took a minute to enjoy the neighborhood I now lived in. People always glorified being raised in the ghetto but one thing for sure, my ass was happy that I no longer lived there. Every house in our community was worth well over a million dollars. Never in life had I thought I would live in a neighborhood like this where there were no corner boys, no jackboys robbing people's shit, no hookers on the corner and no—

"What da fuck? Is that a fuckin' junkie?"

I almost came to a complete stop in the middle of the street when I looked on the sidewalk to my left and saw a man staggering down the road looking completely out of place. He was Black, and in this neighborhood, that alone made you stick out like a sore thumb, but that wasn't even what made him so noticeable. He was dressed in dingy clothes that were much too big. His jeans were torn and caked up dirt collected where his knees should have been. He was wearing an old Obama t-shirt with the words 'Yes, We Can' scrawled across the top and a big, dingy dirt stain circling around them. To keep him warm, he donned a ratty looking, blondish fur coat. Although his skin was chocolate brown, his lips were ashy white, and his unkempt hair was knotted in beady bees that haloed his skull in the style of a beat up Afro. Utterly disgusting and utterly embarrassing.

Frowning as I watched him swagger-walk to a beat that was only in his head, I kept my eyes on him through the rearview mirror until I turned into my driveway, only a few houses down from where he was bouncing down the road. I couldn't *wait* to tell Kane this shit! What in the world was going on in this neighborhood? We paid too much damn money for this shit!

"Heyyyy, Teema! You back already?"

I was so focused on collecting my things so I could run in the house to report my findings to Kane that I didn't even realize my mama was sitting on the front porch.

"Hey Mama, you look good. I thought you said you couldn't watch Kenya because you didn't feel well?"

Cocking my head to the side, I looked her up and down, noticing she was in a much better mood than she'd been when I left. Vibrant even. Don't get me wrong, that was a good thing considering she had Stage 4 Cancer but… it just didn't seem right.

"All I needed was some fresh air, chile. I'm good," she replied.

"You need to check with your doctor to make sure it's okay for you to be sitting outside. It's cold out here."

She started chatting away to me about how she didn't need her doctor to tell her shit because her body let her know what was good for her, and I decided not to even fight that battle with her. Besides, just that quickly, my mind had flowed to other things. Warning signals were going off in my head the more that I thought about the man walking down the street, Cyndy's words at Starbucks, and even Kane's from earlier.

I couldn't get rid of the feeling that I was being dumb and needed to look more into things concerning my mama, but at the same time, I didn't want to. It was like I knew I would stumble upon something I didn't want to believe. And... I hated to admit that I was scared of anything, but it was the truth. I was petrified of finding out that once again, my mama wasn't worth shit.

Janelle

"*T*his slow enough for you?"

I could've punched Luke in the gut.

When I said slow, I meant I wanted to take it slow... between us, as a couple. What I did *not* mean was that I wanted to spend a Friday night at a Bingo hall full of senior citizens.

"5A!" the announcer called out, and I rolled my eyes before covering a space on my card. Lifting my head up, I caught a Black woman who had to be in her eighties, pulling her shirt down, trying to show Luke her pancake breasts. My eyes cut over to him, catching him wink at her. I reached out my leg and kicked him from under the table. That only made him do more. He flicked his tongue out his mouth and then blew her a kiss. The lady immediately started fanning herself. Shit... even I got hot.

"Not everybody wanna take shit slow," Luke said to me, his eyes burning a hole into me as they steadied on my face. I didn't reply. I had no idea what to say.

Once we left there, I beat his ass at bowling, mainly because he refused to take off his Phillip Plein boots to wear the shoes we were given. So instead of bowling comfortably, he rolled the ball with his legs wide to keep from scuffing his shoes, and one hand holding his pants. It was hilarious to watch.

It didn't take too long—after spending night after night with Luke, I had to admit I was tired of taking things slow. I wanted him back. Back in the way that I'd had him before. Also, I was tired of Atlanta. It was nice being home again and having it easy, not worrying about a thing, but living off my father's connections was never where I wanted to be. So after mustering up the courage, I decided to explain this to him one day after work. But then… I lost my nerve and needed a pep talk from my sisters.

"It shouldn't be this hard to talk to him, Jani. You're *grown*. A grown ass woman. Just tell him you're ready to be back on your own." Carmella crossed her arms in front of her chest. Mixie didn't say anything, only looked on while sipping from a cup of juice. The only one missing was TreVonia. She was undoubtedly out with Darnell.

I shook my head. "That's not the hard part. He has already started with dreams of me being his partner… us running the firm together. And then when he's mayor, I'll continue building his legacy. It's his dream and…"

Carmella interjected again.

"I'm sorry to always sound like the selfish bitch, but Daddy is grown too. He's lived out his dreams and it's time for you to live yours. Unless what you want matches what he wants… he'll have to make other plans. And I assure you, he can! Let Darnell run his practice for him!"

I rolled my eyes at Carmella's words but deep down, I knew she was right. She left out of the room after saying everything she'd planned to say and left Mixie and I alone.

"So... you know if you go back to New York, you'll have to finally come clean to Luke."

My heart stopped even though Mixie had only said the same words I'd been thinking myself.

"I know," I replied quietly.

"You ready for that? I mean... I know you wanted to keep things quiet for now." The softness in her eyes gave me a bit of comfort in the midst of my frazzled nerves. It was the reason I'd revealed my secret to her in the beginning.

"No, I'm not ready for that and I intend to continue to keep it quiet. But I know I need to do the right thing and depend on myself. Not Luke, not Daddy, but me. And to do that, I need to get back to work in the city."

"Are you going to tell Daddy?"

Those words had been cycling through my mind for some time now but I already knew the answer. There was no need to even think on it.

"Not yet. I want to wait until I get all my things in order. And... I need to talk to Luke first."

She nodded her head and then walked over and gave me a tight hug. It was exactly what I needed; I knew everything would be all right.

When I approached my daddy's office, I heard him speaking in hushed tones.

"How *dare* you call here and insinuate.... My daughter had nothing to do with any of that and I will not allow you to question her.

Yes, she is an adult! An adult living in *my* house. She wasn't part of a crime. She was a victim and you will not call here insinuating that she or anyone close to her had anything to do with it."

He paused and the room was so quiet that I could hear Pelmington's voice on the other side.

"George, you really don't want to get into the middle of this. As a candidate for mayor, coming in between our pursuit of justice is not something you want to come back to haunt you. Especially with it being done to save your own daughter."

"I'm not running for mayor." Each word sounded like it was torture for him to get out. "That's what you wanted anyways, right? It's always been a competition to you since the beginning. You couldn't stand that I was better than you or that I actually have a chance at being mayor. Well, you got what you wanted. I won't run. Now leave my daughter alone!"

He ended the call and slammed his phone down on the top of his desk. I backed away from the doorway, hoping that I hadn't been seen.

"Janelle."

I should've known that he'd noticed my big ass standing there. No need to hide any longer.

"Yes?"

"What is it that you need?"

Not at all the best timing, right?

Walking in his office, I sat down and tried to ignore the stress in his face. He tried to move past it also by forcing his lips into a smile.

"You don't have to do that, Daddy. I heard the call between you and Pelmington."

"Jani…" He ran his hand over his face in distress and then sighed. "I already know what you're thinking but don't even go there. This thing with Pelmington and I is deep. Real deep. He's a friend on some levels but… there's always been that rivalry."

"But I gave him a way to get the upper hand on you. You're not going to run for mayor and I know that's your dream," I countered, fumbling with my fingers. As much as I loved Luke I couldn't let my decisions to be with him destroy my father's life.

"You didn't give him anything. You're living your life and he's reaching at straws, trying to take down Luke and his brothers any way he can. Just be careful… I don't know if they were involved and I won't ask."

Thank God because I didn't want to lie.

"Just promise me that if anything like that happens again, you'll tell me. We both know I would rather you made different decisions when it came to love."

I flinched. For a girl like me who always made sure to do only the things Daddy approved of, knowing that I was going against his wishes by being with Luke stung.

"But," he continued. "I'd rather not lose my daughter. So I'll respect your decisions. Just be careful and smart."

I nodded my head slowly, knowing exactly what he meant.

"Daddy, I came in here to tell you that I'm ready to go back. Back to New York. I don't want to run from my troubles. I set a goal to make it in that city and I'm determined to do so."

I held my breath as I waited for my daddy to reply.

"I knew you would want to go back and I think you should. As much as I want you here with me, I know you'll do big things in the city. It needs you."

From shit to sugar. That's how my life was going right now and I felt like it couldn't get any better. With my daddy's approval, I was all set to get my ass back in New York and back on my grind. The only problem was that I had to figure out how to keep Luke at arm's reach until I was ready to come clean to him about a few things.

Carmella

"*W*hy do you have to go so soon?"

"Soon?! Mel, I've been here for two damn weeks, sittin' up under your ass and doin' whatever the hell you wanted to do."

"But…" My eyes darted around the room as I started to panic. "It hasn't been long enough."

In the matter of a couple weeks, Cree had easily become my best friend. Duh, you know I wanted more, but he wasn't giving me that at the moment so I just took what I could. It was like spending all of our time together the past couple weeks only made me fall harder for him. I was tired of hiding my feelings but I had to, because every time I tried to make things more than what they were, he pulled away.

"Mel, I'm not going to be with you all the damn time. I don't live here and we're not together. I don't want to be your crutch and you don't need one. You can do this shit on your own."

No, I can't! I thought to myself, but I wouldn't allow myself to utter the words.

"You're stronger than you think," was the last thing he said before leaving for good. He kissed my cheek and got into his car. I watched with tears in my eyes as he rode off down the street. You'd think from looking at my crying ass that he was going off to war. I was devastated but knew I had to move on. Cree was always straight with me… bluntly honest. He was bent on being a friend to me and nothing else, so I had to move on.

Well... maybe I'd practice moving on later because after two glasses of wine—that I wasn't supposed to be drinking, by the way—I was on the phone calling Cree.

"Cree... I know you just left and all but you and I—"

"Yo, are you *drunk?*"

I paused and my thoughts merged. I glanced over at the empty wine glass beside me. I didn't feel drunk... did I sound drunk?

"No, I—I'm not drunk. I just had a couple glasses of wine."

SHIT! Why the hell did I tell him that? Cree knew that I wasn't supposed to have any kind of alcohol at all, and I'd been doing so well until the moment he'd left. Obviously, I wasn't as strong on my own as he claimed I was.

"I mean, I know I'm not supposed to have alcohol but it was just wine," I snickered like I was telling a joke. "But that's not the point. I was thinking about us and how we used to be... I just think that now that I'm well, we should—"

"Mel, stop. There isn't a you and I and damn sure ain't no 'we.' Stop all this beggin' and shit and focus on you. It's not like you to act so desperate for a nigga. The Mel I know wouldn't resort to all this shit when a nigga don't want her. She'd boss up and move the fuck on."

Damn!

My jaw dropped open like my mouth was full of rocks, and I ended the call.

Hours later, I was scrolling through my Instagram page, smiling at the way my notifications were blowing up. It was obvious that I'd been missed during my hiatus. As I was scrolling, I saw a familiar name pop up in the comment section of one of my pics.

Biiiiiiitch! You back and ain't tell nobody! I hate you!

It was Bryan. He was the only person, outside of Daddy and Cree, who knew where I was. Since all of my things were at his place, he worked with Cree to get them sent to Atlanta and would not calm his ass down until Cree told him where I was.

Picking up my phone, I sent a quick message to see if he was able to talk and then gave him a call after he responded. We talked for what felt like hours as he filled me in on the latest and greatest details of his love life. But then, once he was done, he asked the question I dreaded to answer.

"What's up with you and Cree?"

I rolled my eyes. "Not a damn thing. Fuck his rude ass forever!"

"Mmhmm, so the asshole in him has finally resurfaced, huh?"

I sucked my teeth. "It's been out. The shit never left."

"It's the Brooklyn in him, girlfriend." Bryan laughed. "But listen, girl, I've dealt with enough Crees in my time to know that he uses that rude shit to protect his feelings. Don't take him too seriously… at least not what comes out of his mouth, because it's rarely what he really feels."

I heard what Bryan was saying but I wasn't really trying to feed into it. Like Cree's rude ass said, I wasn't no begging bitch and wasn't about to start being one for his ass.

"Since when did you start being the one to dish out decent advice?"

"Since I started seeing my new boo thang, girl! He's an older man and it's made me wise. You should get you one... if you're really done with Cree, that is."

I sensed the doubt in his tone, but I didn't reply because I knew damn well I wasn't really over Cree. The last thing on my mind was another man. Shit! Why couldn't I just forget about him though? It seemed pretty easy for his ass to forget about me!

I put my phone on speaker and listened to Bryan ramble away as I swiped through Cree's old text messages until I got all the way up to our last couple exchanges before he broke up with me.

I love you was the final message he'd sent me. I read it over about ten quick times, loving the tingling feeling in the pit of my stomach that I got from remembering that he'd once loved me and convincing myself that it meant he probably still did.

"Helllloooooo... Carm? You there, girl?" I hadn't even realized that Bryan was calling my name.

"Yeah," I sighed, still looking at the message. "I'm here."

"Well, bitch, I just asked you if you wanted to go out with me. I'll be in ATL next weekend!"

I squealed into the phone and kicked my feet in the air. It was good to be home but everyone seemed to be tiptoeing around me lately. It would be nice to be around a friend who wouldn't treat me like the recovering addict I was, and it would be even better to get back into the party life.

"Hell yes, I wanna go out," I replied back already wondering about what I was going to wear. I had to look fly. Daddy's money could get me back in school but I had to get my Instagram page back popping. There was no way I could depend on him to cover my expenses so I could live my life.

"Just tell me when and I'll be there."

Later on that night, I was in the kitchen making a big ass sandwich that I knew damn well I shouldn't have been eating, when I heard Janelle walk in through the front door. Undoubtedly, her ass was coming back from hanging with Outlaw.

Lucky bitch, I thought as I watched her happy-go-lucky ass prance up the stairs to her room. She was so contently in her own head that she didn't even see me watching her. Don't get me wrong. I was happy for my sister, but I couldn't help being jealous that she was still dating within the Murray crew while I was pining over Cree.

And then something occurred to me.

Leaving my sandwich behind, I ran through the house and out the front door, hoping I could catch Outlaw in time. I ripped through the front door just as he completed his turn out the circular drive and was about to tear down the road to the gate.

"Outlaaaawwww!" I called out, running through the dark towards him. He continued driving slowly away so I took off faster, kicking off my slippers and holding my thin robe in front of me to hide my pajamas.

Seeing I was losing ground, I made a hasty decision. He couldn't hear me or see me and was getting away. So I figured 'fuck it' and dove on the back of his car. He slammed hard on the brakes and my body catapulted forward, hitting the back glass.

"Oof!"

"Carmella? What da fuck?" I heard Outlaw saying after getting out of his car.

I didn't respond. I was still seeing stars. I simply rolled over on my back with my face to the sky as I waited for my vision to return. When it did, I was looking directly into Outlaw's bewildered face. It was obvious he thought I'd lost my damn mind. Hell, maybe I had.

"Your ass better not have dented up my shit, Carmella," he grumbled, plucking me off the top of his trunk rather roughly. I frowned up at him. Only an asshole like Outlaw would be more worried about his damn car than my life.

"Thanks, Outlaw. I'm good, by the way."

"Your ass better be good the way you jumped your monkey ass on my shit. The *fuck* was that about?" He twisted his face up at me and crossed his arms in front of his chest. I was seriously wondering if I had a mental issue even coming out here to ask his rude ass for advice.

"I—I wanted to speak to you about… what the hell you doing?"

I watched as Outlaw used the sleeve of his hoodie to wipe down the back of his car as if I'd dirtied it up.

"The hell it look like? I'm cleaning my shit!" All I could do was roll my eyes.

"Anyways, I was wondering if I could get some advice from you."
I wrapped my arms around my body and let out a deep breath. It was
December in Atlanta... almost Christmas and I was standing outside
in my pajamas with no shoes on.

"'Bout what?"

"About Cree."

It was then that Outlaw finally turned to look at me, still frowning
slightly as he scrutinized the look on my face. Then his eyes dropped
and he noticed me shivering. Without saying a word, he pulled off his
hoodie and handed it to me. It had to be things like this that had Janelle
falling for him. He could go from asshole to gentleman in seconds. It
was hard to hate him.

I wish I could say the same about Cree but he was just straight
asshole... Unfortunately, it was that attitude that I seemed to miss most
about him. He was so hard to understand and so hard to love, but I did
anyways.

"He helped me out... made sure I got clean—"

"Yeah I heard you was hitting that white powder pretty hard. You
sure you over that shit?" Outlaw looked at me skeptically from over the
bridge of his nose and I nodded my head.

"I'm definitely done with it. Even while I was doing it... part of
me didn't want to be so dependent on it, but I didn't know how to
fix my issues. Cree helped me overcome them. But he left me here,
saying that he didn't want to be together and that he just wanted me to
get better. When I asked him not to leave, he said I was begging and
sounded desperate."

I ended what I was saying and waited for Outlaw to respond, but he didn't right away. He only stared at me, his intense eyes pinning me, seemingly burning a hole right through mine.

"Cree said *that?*" he asked finally and I nodded my head.

"Yeah, he said something about me acting desperate for wanting him to stay and wanting us to be together. That was earlier today."

There was a beat of silence that was later interrupted by Outlaw's laughter.

"Yo, he buggin'. Don't let that shit he says fuck with your head."

I narrowed my eyes at Outlaw, wondering why I should believe what he was saying. Why should I continue to be in love with a man who admittedly didn't want me?

"Check this," he said and then pulled out his phone. I waited as he dialed a number and then put the phone on speaker as it rang. A few rings later and the line picked up.

"Yo, what up, bruh?" It was Cree.

"Ain't shit, man. Listen… I just dropped Janelle off at home. She wanna come back to New York but talkin' all this stupid shit 'bout how she don't wanna live together and shit. What's goin' on with you and Carmella? I'm thinkin' I can just cop them a spot and let them live together. I can't have Nell livin' alone."

My heart clenched tightly in my chest as I waited for Cree to answer Outlaw's question. I hated when he called me desperate but, in that moment, I was. I was desperately praying for him to say the right thing… anything that would let me know that he was still feeling me the way I was feeling him.

"I'on know 'bout that shit, bruh. Me and her ain't together no more. She might not wanna come back to the city."

Outlaw kept his eyes on me so I tried not to show the hurt in my face at hearing Cree mention our current relationship status.

"How long you gon' be on that bullshit, nigga? I know you want her ass. Why you actin' like you movin' on or some shit?"

There was a long pause and I felt like with each bit of it, I was dying a little more inside as I waited for Cree to answer. It wasn't until that moment that I realized how much I really loved him... needed him. I felt like if he truly didn't want me that I would be lost. I felt like I would be worthless without his love. And I know that was a fucked up thing to say... I knew I should never determine my worth based on a man, but it was the truth of how I was feeling right then. Cree's love meant that much to me. I needed it in order to go on.

"I'm not movin' on," he said finally. "And I want her. It's just not the right time right now. I need to be sure of some things before we ever got back together. And until I'm sure of that shit, I ain't goin' back to how it used to be."

A sly smile crossed Outlaw's face, and I knew he was satisfied with himself for being able to put my worries at ease. I couldn't hold back a smile either, even if it meant that I had to admit to his cocky ass that he was a genius. Even though Cree didn't want to be with me at the moment, I at least knew he did want me. He still loved me. Knowing that was more than enough for me right now.

"A'ight, bruh. I'll let you handle that shit then and I'll just cop somethin' small for Nell until she get her mind together. After she see that new shit I got, I doubt she'll want to live alone for long."

I raised a brow and stared at Outlaw, wondering what he was talking about and what he had gotten that would have Janelle going back on her plans to live separately. Whatever it was, I knew it was over the top. If it wasn't, it wouldn't be Outlaw.

"A'ight. One, bruh," Cree said and Outlaw ended the call.

"Happy now?"

I nodded, trying to suppress the smile on my face. I knew he saw it anyways.

"Good. Now you can keep ya ass from off nigga's cars and shit," he added and I rolled my eyes as he turned to leave. "Aye, if that college shit don't work for you, you can try ya hand at bein' a stunt double or some shit. I think you'll have that shit on lock."

I crossed my arms in front of my chest and didn't say a word at his sly remark. With one last chuckle at my expense, Outlaw jumped in his ride and tore off down the road to the gate, leaving me wearing his hoodie. Taking it off, I figured I'd return it as soon as I got in the house to tell Janelle about our conversation… and to let her know that Outlaw was planning a little surprise for her back home.

Sidney

"*I*'m just so sick of this shit, Sid. I don't know how much of this I can take. I know he's cheating on me…"

While suppressing a sigh, I rolled my eyes. Faviola was so up and down when it came to her and Tank's relationship that I didn't know what to think. A few weeks ago, she was happy to be in an official relationship with him and now she was convinced he was back to his old games again. I'd been helping Faviola with her man problems since we met and I couldn't keep it up. I had man problems of my own.

"Favi… you and Tank are always going through shit but all you do is take that nigga back. Every time!"

"Sid, it's not like that this time. I really got my heart caught up in this and I feel like I'm being stupid. I—I feel like this nigga done had a baby on me… after we lost ours. He got another bitch pregnant, Sid!"

I crinkled my brow while holding the phone close to my ear while laying back on the bed. I had a few hours before I had to go to work and planned on resting before I went in, but Faviola made sure to put an end to all of that.

"I don't think you should jump to conclusions. Tank hasn't been the most loyal in the past but he knew how tore up you were about the baby and—"

"And he *still* don't give a shit! I lost my baby… he wouldn't even

142

go to the doctor with me when I said I was pregnant, but now this other bitch claiming she's carrying his baby and—I can't even do this with him anymore. I swear."

She really sounded an absolute mess. More of a mess than I'd ever known her to be before. I knew she had feelings for Tank but I had no idea they'd be this strong. Faviola was not weak and definitely not when it came to men. She was a fighter and had always been that way.

My phone beeped and I looked at it to see who was calling. It was Traci. I couldn't help feeling the fire of jealousy burn in the pit of my stomach when my mind flashed back to her and Yolo grinning and smiling in each other's faces. I could've smashed her teeth down the backside of her throat and, had I been a crazier bitch—like the one I was currently speaking to on the phone—I would have.

"… I don't get what this bitch got that I don't have to make him—"

"Favi, I gotta call you back."

"What?!"

"I'll call you back, I promise. And stop jumping to conclusions."

I didn't wait for her to respond before clicking over. I needed to know what Traci had to say and whether it concerned Yolo.

"Hello?"

"Hi, Sidney," Traci replied, her voice much more chipper than normal. I immediately assumed that Yolo had something to do with that and felt myself gritting my teeth.

"I wanted to talk to you about yesterday. I know you told me not to talk to Yolo but I had to. And I'm glad I did because he showed me some text messages from her saying she was leaving the city for good to start a new life on her own. So I guess she really did leave and wanted nothing else to do with me. Or anyone..."

She took a deep breath and I did nothing to fill the silence. Obviously, Yolo had found a way to cover his own ass and I wasn't surprised. The Murray brothers were far from dumb.

"Yeah, I was telling you that. I guess when she's ready, she'll contact you. Just wait on it."

God forgive me.

"Well, I wanted to ask you about something else, too. About Yolo."

I sucked in a breath and sat up straight in the bed, kicking the covers right off my legs. It was official... rest time was over. The last thing I would be getting after this call was sleep.

"What about him?"

My heart thumped in my chest as I waited for her to answer. It was at that moment—that *exact* moment—that I realized I wasn't over Yolo. I would never be over Yolo. I was hurt and afraid of the things I knew he was capable of, but I loved him forever. Always and forever.

"I was wondering... are you over him? Like *really* over him? I mean, you said he was your ex so—"

I snapped.

"Bitch! We broke up less than a month ago," I blurted out before I could stop myself. She had me heated! I knew damn well she wasn't about to ask me about Yolo in order to make herself feel better about trying to get with him right in my damn face. Never mind the fact that her own sister used to date him too!

"Bitch?"

"Yes, 'bitch'! Don't call my damn phone no more wit'cha fake ass. Came here to find your sister but now you satisfied because you found some dick instead. You scandalous bitch!"

I hung up the phone, pressing hard on the 'end call' button and really wishing I could slam it down in her face. For a second, I considered calling Yolo. I had to see if he was really interested in Traci like he seemed to be. My phone chimed and I jumped slightly before answering it.

I'll be a bitch. Yolo's bitch. Just know that he wanted me.

I was seething as I read the message. I knew a lot about Yolo; knew him better than he knew himself probably. Never in life would I have thought he'd give LaTrese's sister some play. But apparently, he was just as much of a dog as his older brother, Tank.

Stomping into the kitchen, I decided to pour myself something strong to drink, topping the liquor off with a cherry to make myself feel fancy, and then I drained the glass. Yolo obviously didn't give a fuck about me so it was time for me to keep it moving. I didn't need to give a fuck about his ass either.

Hours later and I was showing up to work tipsy. After my brother got killed by a drunk driver, I vowed to never drive anywhere tipsy or drunk, so I took a cab to work. When I walked in with my hair straightened down my back, a freakum dress on and my Chuck Taylors—I still couldn't walk in heels—nearly every man around turned their heads to stare. The boyish side of me wouldn't let me wear makeup so I was fresh-faced with the exception of some cherry lipgloss that gave my lips a natural pout. I knew I looked good and the attention proved it.

"Damn!" Mike said as soon as I stepped behind the bar. "You didn't hold back tonight, huh?"

I looked up just in time to see him lick his lips while staring at my legs. I wasn't wearing leggings like I normally did. I had my slim-thick and athletically toned legs on display. Normally, having him react like that to me would have thrown me off, but either the liquor or my anger with Yolo and Traci had me on another level. I felt my cheeks flush with heat and I smiled coyly with my eyes bent as if I didn't see him watching me.

"You look sexy as hell. I mean, you always look good but damn, Sid!"

"I thought it was time for me to do something with this hair. Just because I'm not in a relationship anymore doesn't mean I have to go back to my boyish ways." I shrugged. I did feel more comfortable in my normal tomboy attire, but I had to admit that it did feel good to dress up every now and then. I still couldn't do make up for shit, but wearing a dress and straightening my hair wasn't all that bad.

"Well, I'm damn sure not complaining." Mike licked his lips once more and I felt a tingle in my stomach so I glanced away. The way he was looking at me had me feeling some type of way.

The night went on like normal with us making drinks, but there were some obvious differences in this night than the others before. For one, my tip jar was on fire. Kyle's dumb ass may have been on to something when he said the girls who showed more got better tips, because I was racking up more than I ever had before. And I didn't really have my ass or tits showing either... who knew a tight-fitting, short ass dress and a head full of combed hair could do all that?

The other drastic change was that Mike was touching me more than usual. Not in a disrespectful way but every time he had to walk behind me, I would feel his hands on my hips as he scooted by. He engaged me in conversation between drinks and made sure to keep contact close, sometimes even lightly touching my side as he spoke. Both of us had been taking sips of the leftovers from mixed drinks through the night so we were both feeling the liquor and for Mike, it showed all in his sexy, hooded eyes.

"Can I get ya number, Mama?" a guy asked me when I sat his drink down. He was attractive, not the thuggish type at all, but seemed more like the corporate type. I glanced in his direction and winked.

"I don't know 'bout all that. I'm on the clock."

"But what about when you off the clock?" he persisted.

This time I didn't reply back, just shot him the same smile that had been filling up my tip jar for the better half of the night. I looked to my left and saw Mike watching me. For once, he was seeing me get special treatment from the customers by doing a little flirting, something that I'd watched him do since I met him. He obviously wasn't pleased about it, but I really didn't care. This was about me and my bread... whatever I did to secure that bag was my business, especially if I wasn't doing all that much.

"You need to be careful about leading niggas on like that," Mike whispered to me as I filled up one of the empty bottles of liquor.

"Oh but when you do it, it's just business?"

He furrowed his brow and crossed his arms in front of his chest. "Men and women aren't the same. Men can get the wrong idea when you flirt and don't follow through."

I rolled my eyes, not really feeling anything he was saying. "Yes, Daddy," I sassed and did my best to ignore the annoyed expression on his face. He needed to make up his mind. Either he was going to be probing my body with his eyes or he was going to be acting like he was my damn daddy.

After a long night of work, I counted up my tips and realized that I'd made enough money that night to match everything I'd made the entire week before. Most of it was thanks to the corporate guy who had left me a $100 tip. On it, he'd written his number but I didn't plan on using it. Whoever got the bill next could hit him up.

"Guess I'll see you tomorrow," Mike said as more of a statement than a question. Since Kyle wasn't at work, he was staying a little later to check the building and lock up.

"Yep," was all I said back to him.

I was still pissed off about him trying to condemn me for something he did all the time. Of all people, he should know that I, the girl who dressed like a man for the majority of my life, didn't give a shit about what they said men could do and a woman couldn't do.

"I've been waitin' on you."

Startled, I nearly dropped my keys. Swinging around towards the voice, I peered through the dim lighting to see who it was speaking to me. When I saw it was the guy who had left me the huge tip, I smiled. I was tired as hell and ready to go, but if I could get a repeat customer who would leave me big tips, forcing a smile was worth it.

"Yeah, it's about that time. I'm finally heading out of here," I told him and turned back to open my car door.

I pulled it open but he pushed it back closed, pressing his body in between me and the door. My mouth dropped open and the smile faded from my face. There was something about the glassy look in his eyes that alarmed me. He was definitely feeling the drinks that I'd made for him, but there was something else there that had me on edge.

"You just gon' leave without talking to me? Without givin' me a chance to get to know you? Did you see the tip I left?"

I stammered. "Yes, and thank you but—"

"But?" he frowned and recoiled slightly as if I'd hit him. "But? You think that money didn't earn me a little bit of your time."

Now it was my turn to frown and get attitude to match his cocky attitude. "You can't buy my time like I'm a common hoe. You must have me fucked up."

"And you must have me fucked up! Give me back my damn money!"

He grabbed the upper part of my arm and I pushed him away forcefully. Just like a nigga to put money on the table and automatically think a bitch was supposed to jump for the green. He wasn't a thug but he had the same mentality of ownership that I was not feeling. He thought he owned me just because he gave me a big tip, like that was the entrance fee to my panties.

"I ain't givin' you shit! If you didn't want to leave it, you ain't have to. Ain't nobody beg you for that lil' piece of change!"

"Bitch, you gon'—"

"Bruh, you 'bout to get the fuck out my face," I told him, taking a step back and stepping right back into tomboy mode. I came up around boys, and if need be, I could brawl like one too. Might get my ass beat but I'd at least get a few hits in.

"Is there a problem?"

I turned around and saw Mike walking out, his brows furrowed as he glared at the guy standing right in front of me.

"Naw, playboy, we good," the man replied.

He looked from Mike to me and then back to Mike. It was obvious that he'd already taken in the fact that Mike was bigger than he was, more muscular and definitely more fit. He ain't want none of that and was ready to throw in the cards.

"He was just leaving," I added for him with my arms crossed and gave him a look that dared him to call my bluff.

He glared at me but was smart enough to know that this was the end of our altercation, unless he wanted to start a new one with Mike. He forced out a pressed chuckle and then shook his head in disbelief before walking away.

"He thought just because he gave me a big tip, I was supposed to drop my panties for him or something."

Mike clicked his teeth and shook his head. "I knew somethin' wasn't right about his ass when I saw him. I wasn't tryin' to be your daddy or no shit like that. I just knew that nigga wasn't right."

He came in close to me and ran his hands along the side of my body as he spoke. I damn near melted. It had been a minute since I'd been touched by anyone in this way. Of course, I wanted it to be Yolo but Mike and I had a bond. He was someone I knew, he looked good, and I couldn't ignore the effect that the drinks I'd been sipping from all night had on me.

"I just care for you... always have. Don't want you hurt, you know?"

"Mmhm." I felt my eyes getting heavier the more that he ran his fingertips along the side of my body. It was hypnotizing, especially paired with the scent of his cologne.

When he leaned down to kiss me, I was already expecting it. Wanting it even. I was more curious than anything. I wanted to know if Mike had what it took to make me feel like I did when I was with Yolo. It was something that no other man had been given the chance or opportunity to even show me, because since the moment I'd met Yolo, my heart belonged to him.

Mike enveloped my lips with his, making flutters erupt in the pit of my stomach. I responded naturally, accepting it and letting him in. He deepened the kiss, probing my mouth with his tongue as he cupped my body in his, and I let him. But still... I knew something was off. It didn't feel right.

"I'm sorry," Mike said, breaking our kiss as he pulled away. "I didn't mean to just go in on you like that. I just—I really care about you Sid."

"I know," I whispered and he looked down at me as I shifted from foot-to-foot. I felt awkward in his presence. I didn't know what he was feeling or what he was thinking, but my thoughts were on Yolo. More now than they had been in the weeks before. After experiencing an intimate moment with another man, I knew I wanted him back.

With nothing else left to say, I muttered goodbye to Mike and got in the car to leave. By the time I got home, my head was still spinning and my emotions were in an uproar. Everything in me told me that I was being stupid. It was the same exact warning I'd been hearing for years and years, ever since the day I started dealing with Yolo. But my heart said that I would be stupid not to listen to it. I wanted Yolo and I didn't know how much longer I could ignore it, but I couldn't go on without him.

Outlaw

*A*fter not having a poker night in ages, all the Murray brothers were back together and back in business. This wasn't a private poker game either. This night we had Dr. Mezziani from the pharmacy and a few others joining us. All of them were people in powerful enough places to help us make the moves we needed to make in the streets.

But we weren't dumb... we didn't let just anybody in our circle without ensuring that we had something to hold over their heads. Each one of the people in the room were involved with the Murrays on a business level. They used our services and we used theirs, but the shit that we helped them with could get them locked up for life. It had to be that way in order to cover our asses.

"Tank, you gotta find a way to control ya bitch, man," I spoke up while looking at the cards in my hand. "Her ass said some messed up shit to Grandma, almost got that ass whipped."

"Whipped?" Cree repeated, shuffling through his hands as well. "Whipped, not whooped?"

"Naw, *whipped*. Grandma was 'bout to beat that ass like they did in slavery days," I replied back, and Tank started laughing so hard that he nearly choked on the smoke from his blunt.

"Can't nobody control her crazy ass."

"Y'all together or not? Because it don't seem too smart to be dealin' with her ass on any level if you ain't gon' keep that shit one hunnid. It's obvious that she ain't all there mentally," I added.

Kane frowned and looked at me after he dealt out the last card.

"What da fuck kinda world we live in where Outlaw givin' out relationship advice?" Kane asked with one brow lifted.

"Yeah and especially tellin' niggas to be faithful and shit," Cree chimed in.

"I ain't said shit 'bout bein' faithful. I said that he need to keep that shit one hunnid."

Thorne, a judge that we'd just invited for the first time to our poker games, decided to put his green ass into the conversation.

"Well, might I add, I'd have to put my bid in with Outlaw here. Being straight up is always best. It ensures that you don't have to deal with any bullshit later," he said, trying his best to use the lil' bit of street talk that he'd probably heard from watching a single episode of the show *Power* or something.

"Yeah, what he said," I added, before placing my bid on the game and positioning my stacks on the table. We didn't play for pennies 'round here.

Three games later and I was down bad, about to lose all my muthafuckin' money and ready to pull my piece out on Judge Thorne, because I was convinced his ass was cheating. Everyone else left but Thorne and my brothers, so I figured it was my chance to call his ass out. Niggas would try to call me a sore loser, but fuck all that shit. I wasn't gon' act cool about losin' a game because why should I? Winners ain't do that shit!

"That's some foul shit; how you come in here actin' like yo' ass ain't know how to play the game?" I eyed Thorne so viciously that once his gaze met mine, he flinched slightly before regaining his composure. His eyes rolled from the floor up to the ceiling as he contemplated what he could say.

"You know... you're never supposed to show your hand," he answered with nervous laughter.

My face remained stoic. I wasn't interested in the shits and giggles part of this conversation. I'd never lost a damn game and tonight wasn't about to be the night. Maybe I was overreactin' but a nigga was wound up like a muthafucka seein' as I hadn't had no pussy in a while. Janelle was still on that 'movin' slow' bullshit.

"Hey, I come on friendly terms. I'm just not new to gamblin'." Thorne raised his hands in the air in mock surrender. "If it makes you feel any better, I have some information on ya boy that you might appreciate."

I curled my brow. "My boy?" Shit didn't even sound right coming out his mouth.

"Yeah... Pelmington," he replied, and I widened my eyes. Now he had my attention. Even Kane, Tank, Yolo, and Cree stopped doing what they were doing in order to listen.

"What you got on Pelmington?"

"Something that will even the tables a little. I've noticed he has his mind set on lockin' y'all up for good. Maybe I can help you deal with that situation."

I nodded my head and listened to Thorne speak, telling us all about how Pelmington's ass was an even bigger crook than we were. Apparently, Thorne found out that one of his colleagues had been helping Pelmington obtain guilty verdicts. All that shit that Janelle loved about that nigga was fake. The reason he'd risen to the successful heights that he'd been able to achieve was because he had a conviction rate over 95%, meaning that when he went after a muthafucka, that muthafucka went to jail. However, the reason why wasn't because he was just that good, it was because he had one of the judges in his pocket. Crazy enough, the judge he had in his pocket was also one that I had in mine… and my pockets were much larger than Pelmington's. If I had been just another broke nigga, my ass would be locked up, too.

"That's some crazy shit. You got proof?"

Thorne nodded his head and that was all I needed. Janelle had already told me about how Pelmington was blackballing her pops so that he couldn't run for Mayor of Atlanta. It was one thing for him to fuck with me, but it was something different for him to fuck with my girl and her family.

***

Janelle had a thing for not closing her fuckin' blinds. She was on some white people shit for real. I guess all that time living like her daddy's little princess had her forgetting that her ass was in New York City. And it didn't matter that I made sure her new spot was in a nice, luxurious neighborhood surrounded by the haves instead of the have-nots. Street niggas like me thought of places like this as the perfect lick because of people like her, who figured the neighborhood was so nice they didn't have to take proper precautions.

I was about to head over to Pelmington's to handle some business, but first I wanted to make sure that she was good. From the looks of it, she was. I watched through the blinds as she sat on the brand new cream leather sofa I'd copped her, with her hair in a bun on top of her head, in her grey sweats and tight tank top, pecking away on her laptop as she watched something on TV. Probably *Scandal.* She loved that shit even though I couldn't see why. As much bullshit as she talked about not being able to stand a woman with no morals who couldn't have her own man, she was in love with the Black chick on there and would chew my ass up if I even attempted to down the show.

Chuckling to myself, I pulled off just as I saw Janelle raise a big ass glass of red wine to her lips and take a huge gulp. She was bourgeois as hell but I loved that shit.

Pelmington lived in a big ass townhouse with a security system that was supposed to keep out all the niggas with attitude that he'd ever locked up. A lot of people had a chip on their shoulder when it came to Pelmington so he'd invested a lot of money in making sure that when he was inside the house, they had to stay their ass on the other side. But there was one problem… I had a top notch education that involved being able to hack into a lot of shit. Pelmington's security system being one of those things. In nearly no time at all, I'd been able to not only disarm his system, but also take over his security cameras. I went from room to room searching for him and then…

Bingo.

I found Pelmington but I also found something else, too. I swear life couldn't get any better for me at the moment. Pelmington was definitely home, and I was positive he was in a good ass mood, seeing as he was getting his shit sucked off by the blond chick that Janelle had slapped the shit out of. Grabbing my piece, even though I was positive I wouldn't need it, I stepped out of my rented whip and walked right onto Pelmington's property, pulling my hoody down tight around my head. I figured I wouldn't need all these precautions once I told Pelmington what I had for him, but it wasn't like me to ever be caught slippin'.

"You love how I suck your cock?" the blond chick was sayin' as I crept down the front hall towards the living room where they were conducting their performance. I almost had to chuckle to myself. White chicks always used the word 'cock' and white muthafuckas loved it. The shit seemed funny to me. First bitch to call my shit a cock was getting thumped in the head and told to get the hell on. I was a nigga and we had dicks… I toted around big boy shit.

"Yes. Gobble up my cock, baby," Pelmington replied. This shit was lame as fuck.

"You fuckin' the help, huh, P?" I said finally, stepping out from the dark.

The blond chick screamed and jumped up from where she had been kneeling in front of her boss, who was looking at me like he was about to piss himself. The chick grabbed her clothes and tried to cover herself up, as if I wanted to see her lil' ass titties. Lifting my gun, I released three silenced shots, pumping them into her chest. She slumped over, bleeding profusely from her chest. Pelmington scurried away from her body, moving quickly like a rat.

"SHEEEEIIIIT! What the hell are you d-d-d-doing here?"

Pelmington's face was white as a sheet. Funny how he acted like a straight goon in the courtroom but seeing me up close and personal had him ready to bitch up.

"Yo-you know I'm a district attorney. Killing me carries a mandatory minimum sentence of—"

I shook my head to stop him. Didn't want to hear what he had to say. I wasn't going to kill him. Truth was, if I wanted to get rid of Pelmington, I could have a long time ago. His ass thought he was untouchable, only because we'd allowed him to be that way. Kane had a hard rule against killing certain people who were high profile. He said it would draw unnecessary heat that we didn't need. That was the main reason we kept Pelmington alive... also because we never saw him as a real threat. But I couldn't let him fuck with Janelle and her family, so now I had to intervene.

"Listen, I'mma make this quick. From now on, you're going to leave Janelle Pickney and her father alone. The blackmail and the blackballing... all of that stuff needs to come to an end."

Before he could open his mouth to say another word, I sat down on the chair opposite him and pulled up the emails and evidence given to me by Thorne, proving and detailing the agreement between he and the judge who had helped him illegally put away hundreds of men throughout the past couple decades. Pelmington's expression shifted from shock to surprise to panic but then, like the attorney he was, he quickly collected himself and neutralized his face. It was time for him to try and shake me down so that he could save his own ass. It was a tactic that may have worked for him in the courtroom, but it wasn't about to do shit to me right now. I held all the cards and he had nothing.

Pelmington's lips curled up into a malicious smile and his eyes pulled tight together into a glare that may have been intimidating to the average nigga. I wasn't average though, and I damn sure wasn't scared of his ass.

"You broke into my house and now you want to lay out some rules for me to obey? You came in here and you killed an assistant district attorney right in front of me. You do understand that I could have you locked up for the rest of your life for this, right? The so-called evidence you have is circumstantial at best! Nothing you have is real, tangible proof that I've done anything wrong!"

Pushing my lips together, I gave him a thoughtful look and then nodded my head. "Hmmm, I guess you may be right. So I might as well go ahead and forward this circumstantial evidence over to the Feds and let them do what they do since you ain't worried about the shit."

Pelmington's eyes squinted even tighter than before. "You wouldn't."

With a shrug, I walked over to the phone sitting on a small coffee table near him and grabbed it up. After looking up a number in my phone, I placed the phone on speaker and waited for the other line to answer.

"Hello, you've reached the Federal Bureau of Investigation. This is Maxine, how can I help you?"

"Aye, Maxine, I need to be transferred to someone who can help me out with something. I have evidence that District Attorney Pelmington out of New York City has been—"

"Noooo!" Pelmington squawked like a bird and hobbled over, with his pants still around his ankles, to hang up the line.

Turning to him, I crossed my arms in front of my chest and stared at him without saying a single word. No matter what kind of bullshit that he tried to pull, he knew that I had the upper hand in this situation. My sentence for everything he'd personally seen me do tonight wouldn't have shit on how long they'd throw his ass in prison for what he'd done. Not to mention the additional evidence I'd found showing him taking bribes. He was involved in some corrupt shit, and I knew all about it.

"What do you want?" he asked with his head hanging low between his shoulders. He was broken... right in the exact spot that I wanted him to be.

"Right now, I just need you to leave Janelle and her father alone. But I'll have additional things you can help me with later on. I think we'll be good friends," I told him just as I turned to leave.

"Hey! But wh—what am I going to do about this body? You can't just leave her here!" he shrieked in a high pitch voice that should have only been reserved for bitches.

"You need to get rid of her. And quick..." I advised, ready to drop another bomb on his crooked ass. "Because just in case you pulled some bullshit tonight, I'm going to set up a few emails going from her to you. Initially, it'll look like she was blackmailing you by using the same shit that I found out you were doing. Then it'll go from there to you telling her to meet you here with the evidence she found. I'm not an attorney or nothing but.... Based on those emails and the edited camera footage that I'll have of you leaning over her bullet-ridden body, I'm guessin' they'll try to pin her murder on you."

"Y—you… I—I can't just…What the *fuck* am I supposed to do with a dead body? I don't…Oh God!"

The look on Pelmington's face was priceless. I swear… I was made for this shit.

"You mean you need the Murray brothers to help you?"

He only stood there, stunned and defeated. He'd lost. I'd beaten his ass in the courtroom and now I'd beaten him in this thing called life. Pelmington would not only never again be a threat to me or my brothers, he would actually become a tool that we could use from now on to run the city.

Imagine that.

Teema

I was doing Kenya's hair into braids when the front door opened. I knew it wasn't Kane because he'd just ran out the house stating that something had happened to Tank. From the look of urgency on his face, I wanted to ask him for details but he was out of the house so quickly, I didn't have the chance.

"You look mighty happy. That's how chemo makes you feel?" I asked my mama, scrutinizing her as I slipped some beads on Kenya's braid. YouTube was to thank for my newly acquired skill and, yes, the braids were a little raggedy but I was getting better.

"Girl, to be honest, I'm a little tired but you know… God got me!"

I looked up and let my eyes fall over my mama once more just as she gleefully answered her ringing phone. I didn't know much about chemo, but I knew that people were always complaining about how tired and out of sorts it made them feel.

Not my mama.

In fact, she looked better than she had ever looked since she'd started staying with me. She was dressed in the nice name brand clothes I'd bought her, along with the jewelry and pricey shoes she'd begged for. If my mama was living her last days, I wanted her to have everything she wanted and more. Well… she definitely had everything she wanted but her ass did *not* look like she was living her last days.

"Yeah, girl, lemme call you later," she said to whoever it was on the other line. Funny how now she had friends. Where were they when her ass needed help?

"Mama, when you gon' have your doctor call me? It's been weeks and I haven't heard anything from him."

She placed her hands on her skinny hips.

"Well, the doctor is a very busy man, Teema. I'm sure he has better things to do than to talk to you about my business."

Something about the way she said it made me wanna two-piece her sick ass but I stayed in my seat. I was the one paying Dr. Ochobe's ass his lil' copay every time she went down to his office, so for her to act like he was too busy to talk to me had me about to flip.

"How's he not too busy to take my money but can't give me a call?"

"Is that what this is about? Money?"

Her attitude was a little too much for somebody who had been begging me for a place to stay only a couple weeks ago.

"No, it's about me needing to know what's going on. You said the doctor was going to call me about your diagnosis and he needs to do it."

With a twirl of her eyes, she stalked away, going up the stairs to her room. I continued to finish up Kenya's hair, but I still had a feeling that something wasn't right. Then my mind went back to the man I'd seen walking out of my neighborhood the other day. It was obvious he had been on some sort of drugs. What he was on, I didn't know, but he damn sure was on something.

After finishing up Kenya's hair, it was time to bathe her and get her in the bed. After she finally fell asleep, I took a shower and got in the bed myself. Kane hadn't called me back yet so I didn't know what was going on with him or Tank, but I knew it was serious and didn't want to bother him. I ended up falling asleep watching a show I loved about flipping homes for a profit. In another life, that's what I would have chosen to do for a living.

I woke up to the sound of voices, mainly a deep voice, and that's what put me on alert. Sitting right up in the bed, I froze and honed in on the voices, trying to pick up who it was. It didn't take me long to pick up on Kane's deep, throaty tone, and I immediately moved to get up and run downstairs to ask him what was going on. But then I picked up on my mama's voice and something about her tone alarmed me. Creeping to the edge of the doorway and then a little down the stairs, I made sure to be absolutely still as I listened to their conversation.

"You gotta stop with dis bullshit. I mean it. What'chu gon' do if I tell Teema?"

"You ain't gon' tell Teema shit because you know she ain't gon' believe you. Now stop actin' like you don't want this pussy, nigga. I been seein' the way you been lookin' at me," my mama said and I almost gasped out loud, not believing the words that I was hearing come out of her mouth. What in the entire fuck?

"Man, put some fuckin' clothes on and close your damn legs. The only reason I don't tell Teema 'bout this bullshit you pullin' is because I know it'll kill her to know that you on some fuck shit. But she'll find out 'bout your scheming ass. Bet," Kane replied and I could feel from his tone that he was really trying to keep himself from going off.

I crept a little closer to the edge of the stairs and saw a sight that I never wanted to see in my life. Kane was standing up with his duffle bag on his back as if he'd just walked in the house, and he was facing my mama who was sitting on the floor ahead of him, legs spread eagle, showing off her clean-shaven vagina. Her robe was open, exposing her pancake chest as well. I wanted to puke; I was just that disgusted.

"I'm dyin'. Give me some of that good dick before I meet my maker."

In a flash, Kane took a gun out and held it to his side, cocking it with a click. "I can make your ass meet him sooner if you don't get da fuck up."

The sound of the gun must have brought her to her senses because in a flash, she was on her feet and pulling her robe together while giving him a sharp look as if she couldn't stand him.

"Fuckin' junkie," he muttered, glaring at her. "The sooner your daughter finds out about your ass the better."

I was stunned into silence. If this had been any other woman, I would have marched down there and beat the shit out of her, but it wasn't just any other woman. This was my mama and I was shocked to the point where I could barely move. I backed away from the stairs and ducked back into my room, closing the door behind me. When I looked down at my hands, they were shaking uncontrollably. My skin was hot and I felt like I couldn't breathe. What the hell was going on in my house?

It took about ten minutes for me to come to terms with what I'd seen and heard before I got mad as hell and snatched my bedroom door open. First, I stormed down the stairs to see what Kane was up to but when I got to the living room, he was gone. Most likely, he was in his private room where he went to get himself together after coming home from dealing with whatever he had put up with in the streets. It was like a cleaning process for him, a detox that he needed before coming up and being the family man that he needed to be for Kenya and me.

Since he was gone, I turned my attention to confronting my mama's nasty ass and went right back up the stairs. When I stormed into her room, I noticed the shower was on in the adjoining bathroom but I didn't give a shit. I was ready to pull her black ass right from out of the water and beat her like she stole something. But then... something on her dresser caught my eye.

It was a box of baby wipes. Normally, this wouldn't be a big deal being that Kenya used baby wipes and she was her grandmother. But the fact that she never watched Kenya for me and had definitely never changed a single diaper, made this situation a little different. Walking slowly over to the wipes, I grabbed the box in my hand and shook it after realizing that it seemed a lot lighter than it should have been. The contents rattled like coins were inside.

When I pulled the lid open, I wish I could say that I was surprised about what I saw. There was a syringe, and a small bag of a substance that I knew were drugs. There was also a rubber band, some pills, an old credit card and a powdery substance, along with some money rolled up in another rubberband. This bitch had been using my coins to get high! It was immediately obvious to me that the money that was in the box was definitely the same bills I'd been giving her to pay for her doctor visits. Her fake ass doctor visits anyways.

"What are you doin' in my shit?!"

I didn't even realize that the shower was off and the bathroom door was open until I heard her voice coming from my side. Whipping around, I settled my eyes on her, knowing that the fire from them was radiating through. She seemed unaffected by my anger and just stood in front of me with an attitude of her own.

"Your shit? You used the money I gave you to buy drugs and brought them into my house, and you're worried about me going through your things?"

She lunged for the box in my hands and I stepped back out of her reach.

"Give me back my shit!" she screamed, and I squeezed my eyes closed for a brief second.

I will not beat her ass. I will not beat her ass. I will not beat her ass.

The thought continued on in my mind and it was the only thing that kept me from jumping on top of her. As much as I hated this bitch that was in front of me right now, I didn't want her to take me back to the place and the person I used to be. I'd grown beyond that and I wouldn't resort back to who I was.

"I said, give me my shit, you stupid bitch!"

On second thought, yes I would.

Stepping forward, I cradled the wipes box in one hand and then slapped the shit out of her face with my other hand. She lunged for me once more, dropping her towel, and jumped right on me. I fell backwards, releasing the box, and tried to push her away but she was wet and slippery. She started pelting me with punches, and even though I didn't want to hit her back, my instincts stepped in and I started defending myself, knocking her in every part of her body that I could come into contact with.

I heard heavy stomps and then her door swung open. I tried once again to push her off of me, but she grabbed onto my hair and yanked hard as hell, bringing tears to my eyes.

"Da fuck is goin' on in here?" Kane yelled out and then reached down, plucking my mama from off of me and tossing her towards the opposite wall. I yelped out loud, feeling a few strands of my hair going along with her.

"She needs to get the fuck out of my house! NOW!" I screamed.

Looking over at her, I swear I wanted to spit in her face. She was ass naked and sitting in the corner with her arms crossed and a smug look on her face. Yeah, she'd won. Even though she was being kicked out now, she'd conned me into letting her live like a celebrity for the past few weeks.

Kane grabbed me and hugged me tightly in his arms, trying to calm me down as I cried. I felt his lips against my forehead and loved the feel of his kiss, but I still was so enraged and felt so stupid that I could barely think. How could someone have a mama as wicked as mine? I wondered sometimes how my life would be if she'd been the one to die instead of my daddy. Maybe I would've been happier but maybe not. Maybe I would have never met Kane.

"Go back to bed, bae. I'll get her out of here," he said and I tried to ignore how my mama licked her lips seductively from behind his back. I swear I hated her ass. She was all evil and deserved an academy award for tricking me the way she had. It was all fake and I knew it. The cancer, chemo, everything… she was the ultimate bitch.

"All her shit in here can go. I don't want any of it left… even the money. She can kill herself gettin' high off that shit for all I care."

Kane nodded his head and released me so that I could walk out of the door. Before leaving, I paused and took a good look at my mama, knowing it was the last time I would see her. For the rest of my life, I never wanted to lay eyes on her again. I wanted this to be the last time and I had to let her go for good. Her evil glare cut into mine and she raised her lips into a sneer before barking at me like a ferocious animal. I jumped and she laughed like it was the funniest thing on Earth. Her mind was gone. She was crazy, and it was a shame I was only just now noticing it.

About an hour later, she was gone and Kane came into the room. I was sitting up on the bed, unable to sleep and unable to rest. I had tears in my eyes because I was totally devastated about what all had gone down tonight. Never had I thought things would end like that. I guess I was being stupid in some people's eyes, but it wasn't that. I was hopeful. I was hopeful that, even if it was her last days, I could have the mother I'd always wanted. The kind of mother that was my best friend, like so many other people had.

"She gone?"

Kane nodded his head and sighed. "Yeah... she's outta dis bitch."

In spite of my feelings, I smiled at his choice of words.

"Good," I replied. There were a few beats of silence and then something came to mind.

"What happened with Tank? Is everything okay with him?"

Kane's eyes came to mine and the sadness in them made my chest tight. I couldn't take any more surprises tonight. I couldn't take any more bad news... no more heartbreak.

"He's fine—"

"Oh, thank God!" I blew out a breath of relief. But when I looked back up at Kane, I knew there was more to be said. The worst part of his statement was still left unsaid.

"It's Faviola..."

"Faviola?" I asked, squinting my eyes at Tank. "His girlfriend? What's wrong with her?"

Kane sighed deeply and sat on the bed, running his hand over the top of his head.

"She's gone."

"Gone?" I parroted, not entirely sure what he meant.

"Yeah... she's dead."

Janelle

"*I* can't believe she's gone. Is Sid okay? Have you spoken to her?"

I was back in New York, in my new apartment. Carmella decided she needed a break from life and came with me to help get me packed. Or at least that's what she said. I felt like she was still holding on to the idea of getting back together with Cree. Deep down, I wanted them together.

I'd never seen Carmella so torn up over not being with someone before. She usually carried herself as the prize in whatever relationship she was in—which, she was the prize. But the difference was she never thought of a guy as being anything other than an option. To see her actually trying to be with someone because she wanted him in her life was a good change.

"I did speak to her... she's torn up about it. She said that Faviola had been calling her about Tank and wanted to talk about all the stuff that she was going through, but she was too busy doing her own thing."

"Sid can't fault herself for having her own issues. It happens. Everyone has a life and sometimes they get too busy to deal with..."

My voice faded off when I realized that I was talking about myself even more than Sidney. I'd been so busy with my own shit that I'd totally forgot about Carmella and what she was going through. I still felt disappointed in myself about that.

"Yeah, that's true, but it's hard to not blame yourself when your best friend kills herself."

I paused and grabbed a box of my things, pulling each piece from the box as my mind turned. Carmella was quiet as well and I wondered if she was thinking the same thing that I was.

"Are they sure that she killed herself? I mean, Tank was with her, right?"

Carmella sighed and rolled her eyes. "The story is that he came over and she confronted him about some girl. They argued and he admitted that he'd gotten some other bitch pregnant during the time that she was going through the loss of their baby, and that he planned on being in this baby's life. Shit got crazy and she took the gun and killed herself..."

That was some sad stuff right there. I really didn't even know what to think, but I knew that if something like that had happened between Outlaw and me, I'd be torn up about it. I was certain that I wouldn't kill myself, but I couldn't judge Faviola for the decision she'd made no matter how much I wished she hadn't. We had two different paths and two different lives. She felt like she had nothing else to live for and was tired of people treating her as an option. As much as I wished she had reached out to someone to convince her otherwise, I couldn't change the past.

"I didn't know her that well and, to be honest, I didn't like her, but it's sad anyways."

Carmella nodded her head before lifting her eyes and focusing on me. "You okay? You look a little sick in the face."

Reaching up, I rubbed at the sweat beads that seemed to have suddenly sprout up on my forehead. To be honest, I felt like shit.

"I don't feel good," I replied, just before my stomach made a vicious twist that sent me running to the bathroom. I made it in there just in time to throw up all of the tuna sandwich and chips that I'd just made for Carmella and I to eat. It was good going down but nasty as hell coming up.

"Damn, Jani! You okay?" Carmella asked me just as I walked out of the bathroom after rinsing my face and brushing my teeth. Her face was buried in her phone, so I knew that although she was saying the right things, she really wasn't the least bit worried about my response, which was a good thing. I didn't need her asking me too many questions.

"Are you still keeping up with your Instagram page? I've noticed I haven't had to be your personal photographer lately."

Carmella's face shifted with my words and I began to worry that I'd said something wrong. I knew something strange was going on between her and Cree, and that they weren't together at the moment, but I wasn't stupid enough to believe they were done forever. One thing about Cree that I knew, was that he was just as stubborn as she was, but everyone could tell how he felt about Carmella just by seeing the way that he looked at her. He wasn't going anywhere and neither was she. I guess kinda like me and Outlaw.

"Cree never liked it," she blurted out and I lifted a brow, knowing that she hadn't meant to bring up Cree's thoughts on the matter. About a second later, she noticed what she'd said and hurried to correct it.

"I mean... not like I give a damn what he thinks about the shit *I* choose to do with *my* life. But he made some points about it that I agree with. It's time for me to grow up and get serious about my life. I kept saying that I was using my pics on Instagram as a way to become a model but I wasn't actively pursuing a modeling career. I just liked all of the attention I was getting. And the special treatment."

Duh.

I rolled my eyes. The only person convinced that Carmella was showing her ass as a means to a real career, was Carmella. She'd always been the one who was addicted to attention and she lived by the motto 'if you got it, flaunt it.' Getting a job with Zeke to model for his company was about the closest she'd come to making her 'modeling' a real career and, well... you see how that ended.

"I plan on going back to school and focusing on my degree. I want to still do some sexy shit because... look at me." She framed up her body as if to demonstrate that she was obviously too sexy to not do some sexy shit. "But, at the same time, I want to be respected... like you are."

Couldn't help the smile that took over my face. After all the bullshit that I'd been through the past few months, the last thing I thought was that I was someone worth respecting.

"You know he loves you, right?" she said suddenly, pulling me out of my thoughts. Squinting, I searched her eyes for further explanation as to what she was talking about.

"Outlaw... Luke. That man is crazy over you. Just don't mess it up."

"Me, don't mess it up?" I cocked my head to the side and pointed at my chest. "I'm definitely the easiest one to get along with out of the two of us."

Carmella widened her eyes and shook her head doubtfully.

"Um, no. Outlaw is definitely easier to deal with than you. I'm no longer a gangsta's chick since Cree and I aren't together—" I rolled my eyes at her. "—But one thing I do know, is that if you're going to be with Outlaw, you have to be smarter about this street shit. You got the common sense but when it comes to the street life, you're about as smart as a brick."

I took immediate offense to her words and frowned. If I was as smart as a brick when it came to street shit, what did that make her?

"When did you become the expert on dating a thug?"

She lifted one brow and gave me a straight look, no smile in sight. "Let's just say I learned a lot of things in rehab."

Carmella was dramatic as hell. Pursing my lips, I stood up to pick up my things and head on to my bedroom so I could go over some business stuff I needed to review in order to get my new law office off the ground and running. I was done with the conversation, even though I knew she was right. If I was going to be the woman that Luke needed, I had to know what I was getting myself into and act accordingly if I was going to make it as the woman by his side.

"Well, goodnight, Carmella. And thank you for your knowledge." Yes, I definitely rolled my eyes hard on the word 'knowledge.'

"Wait... one more thing," Carmella yelled out, just before I was about to close the door to my luxurious master bedroom.

"What?"

She cut her eyes at me and gave me a half-smirk that transformed into a devilish grin.

"Your little secret that you're keeping from everyone—the one you think only you know about—I've figured it out."

My mouth dropped open when I saw the motion she made with her hand, proving that she did actually know the exact thing I'd been hiding.

"And if *I've* figured it out that quickly, you may want to tell Outlaw. He's no dummy so he'll figure it out, too."

She walked away with her smug ass smirk still intact, leaving me looking and feeling like an idiot because I knew that she was most definitely right.

Janelle

$\mathcal{A}$ few days after my conversation with Carmella, I was in my brand new office working. I didn't have any cases at the moment but there was still a lot of work to be done in order to get clients. I had to advertise my practice and get at least one legal aide on my team to help me out. There was a lot that came with legitimizing a business that I hadn't considered.

I was taking the last bite of my turkey and cheese sandwich when the door opened up and in walked Luke, dragging a younger boy inside with him. The boy looked no older than eighteen years old and like he'd been roughed up a bit. Behind Luke was his brother Yolo, who I hadn't spoken to all that much but couldn't help being a little intrigued by based on what I'd heard from Sidney. He leaned on the wall, dressed head to toe in red and white, matching all the way down to his shoes and socks. Out of his pocket stuck out a red and white bandana.

"Luke… what are you doing?"

He tossed the boy he'd dragged into my office roughly to the side. He hit the wall with a loud bump that even made me flinch. Luke walked over and kissed me deeply, cupping my ass as if we were the only ones in the room. I took in a deep breath, loving the smell of him as well as the feel of his body pressed against mine. I was lost in him, and it wasn't until Yolo cleared his throat that I remembered we weren't the only ones in the room.

"This stupid ass muthafucka over here is my lil' homeboy, Beanz," Luke explained, pointing at the teenage boy who was sitting in the corner, a sour look on his face from being referred to as a 'stupid ass muthafucka.'

"He got picked up on some stupid shit… open container or some bullshit like that. But the fuckin' cops ran his prints and connected him with an armed robbery they been investigating. So…" Luke turned to me, crossing his arms in front of his chest. "You got ya first client outside of the Murrays."

My eyes widened as I looked from him to the teen boy who was still putting his ass dent in my fresh new carpets. If they had matching fingerprints, this was probably an open and shut case. What in the world could I do to help him?

"Empty ya fuckin' pockets, nigga!" Luke yelled out to the boy who looked like he was about to run straight up the wall. "My lady don't work for free!"

Beanz reached into his pocket and pulled out a wad of cash, much bigger than anything I'd ever seen anyone carry on them at one time. Luke snatched it out of his hands and then pushed it into mine.

"Deposit for your services, ma'am," he said with a cocky smile, playfully using a lil' bit of the southern twang he kept hidden for the most part. "Yolo, take this nigga back in the conference room to wait for us to get in there so he can start talking."

Yolo nodded his head and silently walked over to Beanz, snatching him up from the ground as if he couldn't walk for himself.

The boy scowled at being tossed about and Yolo popped him on the back of the head.

"Get ya attitude in check, nigga. You lucky we ain't let ya reckless ass sit in county for this bullshit," he told him, instantly making him straighten up.

Luke laughed as he watched their interactions, and I couldn't help but give off a half-smile of my own. The Murray brothers didn't play around. It was still crazy to me how they could go from thug to jokester in a matter of seconds. I'd always been told Yolo was the sensitive, light-hearted one but the last couple times I'd seen him, he was anything but. Today, he was roughing up a teenager and the last time I'd really interacted with him, he'd been threatening Chris... who had disappeared off the face of the Earth.

"When you packing this shit up so I can take you to dinner?" Luke asked me, sitting on the top of my desk.

He grabbed me and pulled my body in between his legs. I felt my entire body get warm from being so close to him, between his legs... feeling the hardness of him poking me through his jeans. I cleared my throat before I could answer.

"I can be out of here in a couple hours—"

"Make that 30 minutes," Luke interjected, kissing me on the lower part of my neck. He cupped his hands in front of me, holding first my stomach before traveling one hand up to my breast and the other down between my thighs. I immediately forgot where I was and leaned into him, parting my thighs and closing my eyes.

"30 minutes?"

"Mmhm," he whispered into my ear. "Go to my spot after work. I'll have someone there to get you ready for what I have planned tonight. It'll take some time for me to prepare so just put them hammerhead toes in the air and let them chicks I hired do what I paid them to do."

Smiling, I elbowed him in the ribs. But deep down, I was excited about whatever Luke had planned. Everything about him was over the top. I had a feeling that tonight wouldn't be anything different.

***

"Are you going to tell me what you have planned?"

It was hours later and a lot of pampering later too. My hair was done, which was a good thing considering I'd been well overdue for a wash and set. Luke made sure that everything from my hair to my nails and feet were taken care of and even arranged for some outfits to be brought to his house for me to choose from.

Now I was all dressed up with my hair curled around my shoulders and my ankle length Chanel gown on. I felt beautiful. It was crazy how I went so long feeling like I was the ugly, smart sister, but every day with Luke he made me feel like the most gorgeous woman on the planet.

"You ready?" Luke said from behind me.

I turned around and my eyes fell on the sexiest man on this side of heaven. Hands muthafuckin' down! I don't care who you think you might be datin', engaged to or who is wifin' you up, he ain't got *nothing* on Luke Murray, and that's a fact. I had to take a breath before I answered because I was so caught up on his black custom-made, designer suit that he'd paired with an emerald green dress shirt to match my dress. Teema must have braided up his hair at the last minute because his shit was on *fleek* as the kids say. Bling in his ears and on his wrists, side burns going down his face, running into his goatee… he was *all* that.

"I'm ready."

"No, you're not," he told me and I lifted one brow at him.

That's when he reached out, revealing a beautiful diamond and gold tennis bracelet. He draped it around my wrist and clasped it. Now mine was shining about as bright as his. I was about to scream when I got a good look at it, but then I noticed he'd rotated behind me and was placing a matching necklace around my neck. Lastly, he pulled out some diamond teardrop earrings and placed them in my bare ears.

"Now you're ready," he told me, and I could barely speak from looking at myself in the mirror behind him. I was shining bright like a diamond. Hell… like about a hundred diamonds.

After driving for a while, my stomach started to stir and my mood shifted slightly. I couldn't help but think about the secret that I was holding from Luke. Every moment I spent with him was magical but then there were these moments that I was reminded that I wasn't living life on the up and up. I was keeping something from him and I needed to tell him. Maybe the time was now.

I quickly changed my mind. We were being chauffeured and I definitely didn't want a third party in my business. Plus, Luke had something nice planned and I didn't want to change the mood.

"Shit!" Luke cursed all of a sudden, right when I was thinking about the one thing I was holding from him. "I left something at your office earlier. We gotta swing by and get it."

I nodded my head and then fell back into silence, looking out the window next to me. I could feel Luke's eyes on me and I knew I needed to get myself together. I didn't want to talk to him about what was going on in my head because it wasn't the time. It was better if I told him later on tonight. There was no point in ruining our good time.

We pulled up to my office and I took a deep breath. Luke hesitated before getting out and that's when I remembered that I had the keys. Reaching in my purse, I pulled them out and handed them over to him.

"You know what? Come in with me. Let's just take a quick walk inside. I wanna get you alone really quick." He licked his lips and there was an instant throbbing in my middle.

"You nasty."

"So?" he replied back. Quick ass mouth.

We walked to the door and Luke took forever to open it, but it was okay because my nerves were still on edge. Finally, the door was open and we walked inside of the dark building.

"I'll get the light," Luke said just before I went for it and he flicked it on.

"SURPRISE!"

As soon as the lights were on, my eyes landed on a huge group of people standing in front of me. When I was able to adjust, I recognized my daddy, my sisters, Tayesha and some other friends and family from back in Atlanta. I was even able to pick out Teema, and Luke's brothers, all except for Yolo. What was going on?

Luke kissed me on the cheek and grabbed my hand. "Welcome to your office warming party, bae. I hope this ain't too much but you deserved it. I want everyone to share in your accomplishments."

He kissed me again as I looked around the room at all of the décor that read 'Congratulations, Janelle.' This was all for me? Whoa… it was insane. I definitely wasn't expecting it, but it was probably the sweetest thing anyone had ever done.

"I can't take all the credit," Luke continued. "Your sister, Mixie, helped me out a lot with planning this and deciding to do it." I smiled over at her and she smiled and waved back. "Go 'head and chill with your fam."

I did just as Luke suggested and ran over to my sisters, hugging them all. They all knew about this and were able to keep it a secret. Even TreVonia's loud mouth ass. It was a damn miracle.

"Congrats, sis! This shit is *dope*. Can I get a job?" TreVonia asked and I rolled my eyes. She had never been able to keep a job longer than a couple weeks… maybe a month. It was a running joke amongst the family.

"I'm proud of you," Mixie said, reminding me so much of my mother that it brought tears to my eyes. She hugged me and Carmella joined in, squeezing me tight like I hadn't spent most of the morning with her.

"Janelle," my daddy's voice boomed through my ears. When I released my sisters and spun around to look at him, he was standing with Tayesha at his side, both of them beaming with huge smiles. Something about how close there were standing to each other piqued my curiosity, and for the first time I thought about how cute of a couple they would make.

"I'm so proud of you, baby," he told me and Tayesha nodded her head by his side. "You have a beautiful place here and I know you've got a beautiful start ahead of you. Luke really did everything he could to make this special for you."

Smiling, I nodded my head in thanks and then watched as he and Tayesha walked away. He grabbed a drink from one of the waiters walking around and handed her one before taking one for himself. Both of my brows rose up in the air.

"Oh, he's definitely hittin' that, if that's what you're thinking," TreVonia announced. Mixie jabbed her in the side with her elbow, but I caught it.

"You—you think they are a couple?" I asked her.

"Not *think*, we *know*," TreVonia added, ignoring Mixie who was cutting her eyes at her. "They are definitely dating. Daddy thinks he's doing a good job of keeping it under wraps, but I'm not stupid."

"No, you're just nosey," Mixie piped up and rolled her eyes.

"Whoa," Carmella and I both said, looking back at Tayesha and Daddy. Yeah, they definitely did seem to be a couple. And I couldn't say that I was mad about it either. I loved Tayesha. She'd been the closest thing to a mother that we had since losing our own.

I worked the room, thanking everyone for coming but the entire time, I felt Luke's eyes on me. A few times I caught his stare, and he would only smile a little before turning away. But there was something in his eyes that made me feel like he was up to something. It took a little while but eventually I found out exactly what it was.

"Aye, Nell… let me holla at you for a minute." He came over and grabbed me by the elbow just as I was finishing up some small talk with one of my dad's old friends who I hadn't seen in a while. I politely said goodbye and then turned to Luke.

"You okay?" I asked when I noticed how nervous he looked. My stomach flopped around when I wondered whether or not he'd found out my secret before I'd had the chance to tell him. Oh god… what if he did? That would probably be the worst thing that could happen right now. I needed to be the one to tell him first.

"Nell," he started, darting his eyes around. He had one hand in his pocket fumbling with something. "I just want to tell you how much I love you. The past few months, we been goin' through some straight bullshit. We missed out on our first Christmas together… New Years… all of that over some bullshit. But during all that, I realized that I never wanted to spend another holiday or special moment without you. Not ever."

He paused and wiped his face with his hand. He seriously looked like he was about to pass out. What the hell was wrong with him? Using my lawyer instincts, my brain started to work. I assessed his stance, his tone, his words and finally, the fidgeting he was doing in his pocket. And that's when it dawned on me.

Oh shit! Noooo, he's about to propose!

"Nell, I—shit, I gotta get this out," he said to himself, visibly shaken by what he was trying to do. I put my hands up to stop him.

"No! Don't, Luke!"

He frowned deeply at me and I knew then that I couldn't wait. I had to come clean and tell him what I'd been keeping before we got too far along and things began spiraling out of control. Looking around, I realized that I couldn't come clean in front of this crowd. I grabbed him by his hand and pulled him out of the main room and into my private office.

"What's going on?" he asked as soon as I closed the door behind him.

"I—I, um…" Now I was the nervous one. "I have to come clean to you about something. I've been keeping a secret and… I think you're about to propose and I can't let you do that without saying what I need to say."

Furrowing his brow, Luke crossed his arms in front of his chest and trained his eyes on me. He pushed his lips into a straight line but didn't say anything, only waited for me to continue.

"I—I'm…"

Pause. Pause. Pause.

My mouth went dry, I allowed my eyes to travel around the room, I shifted in my shoes… basically, I did every damn thing I could think of to stall. And stall and stall.

"Nell, get dat shit out!" Luke barked. And that's when I figured… what the hell? Just blurt it! So I squeezed my eyes shut and just let it out.

"I'm pregnant!"

There was silence for a minute. Then two minutes. Finally, I opened up my eyes to peer at Luke and I was met with a big ass smile.

"For real?" he asked and I took a breath. The first that I'd been able to take since blurting out my announcement.

"Yes... I found out the day I decided to move back home. I've been keeping it quiet because I didn't want it to influence your decision to be with me, and I wanted to be sure that I really wanted you in my life, too."

"Da hell you mean? You got my shorty in you, you my baby mama so you ain't got no damn choice. Talking 'bout you had to be sure you wanted to be with me... the hell you think this is?"

I rolled my eyes at Luke's authoritative tone. He thought he called all the damn shots.

"Yes, I understand that but I—"

"Ain't no buts," he concluded on his own. "Shit... you really pregnant?" He didn't even wait for me to answer before he jumped up and punched his fist into the palm of his other hand. "I *knew* your ass would get pregnant as soon as I let you ride in my front seat. That shit is the truth and I keep tellin' niggas that shit! At first, I was wonderin' because it's been a minute, I damn sho' been hittin' that and you still wasn't gettin' fat and shit, but I *knew* it was bound to happen. Damn!"

I rolled my eyes again. I didn't know what the hell he was talking about, but I figured it was his ego doing the talking so I kept my peace.

"So what you say then?" he asked, finally looking back at me.

"About what?"

He walked close to me and pulled out a black box from his pocket. I held my breath, but when he opened it and revealed the beautiful teardrop yellow diamond inside, I gasped hard.

"About this. You gon' marry me or not?" he inquired, cocking his head to the side. "I mean, I was gon' get on my knees and shit but since you already know—"

"I—I don't want to be married now," I told him, honestly. It was what I felt but I hadn't expected the words to come out so easily.

"What? You don't want to marry me?" The hurt in his voice was hard to ignore. I shook my head and grabbed his hand.

"No... I'm not saying I don't want to marry you. I just don't want to get married *now*. And I don't know when I'll think it's the right time, but I've given up a lot these last few months and I'll continue giving up more for the baby. But one thing I don't want to give up is my career and being my own person. I want to understand who I am and become the woman I need to be before being a wife. I want to marry you, but I need to wait until I get my dreams in order. I have this practice and I want to dive into it and be successful on my own first... I need you to understand that."

Luke sat down on the top of my desk and licked his lips. Then a thoughtful expression crossed his face and he began massaging his beard with his fingers.

"I can dig it," he said quietly. "But I still need you to wear this ring. You can wait as long as you want before you pick that wedding date, but you wearin' this ring and you *will* be my wife."

I guess that was as close as I was going to get to a compromise.

Smiling hard, I put out my hand and let him slide the beautiful ring on my finger. I didn't know when, but I would be Mrs. Murray someday. Luke had demanded it and I had no other choice but to agree with his cocky ass.

"One thing… don't tell anybody about the baby just yet. I wanna tell my dad separately first."

He looked like he was going to object but then nodded his head. "That's your choice."

We started to walk to the door of my office so that we could join the crowd but before we could step outside, Luke pressed his hand to my chest, stopping me before he opened the door.

"This room sound proof, right?" he asked and I nodded.

With his hands out, he yelled loudly, "We're gonna have a muthafuckin' babyyyyyy!"

My eyes bugged out of my head and Luke looked at me, smiling, before shrugging.

"I just had to get that shit out."

I shook my head and laughed as he held the door open for me to exit first, still not quite believing the direction my life was taking. Luke squeezed my hand tightly as we walked back into the crowd and mouthed 'we're going to have a baby' when I looked at him. Smiling, all I could do was roll my eyes. I mean, what else could I do when it came to Luke 'Outlaw' Murray? After all, he was about to be my baby daddy… which meant I had to deal with him for the rest of my life, as he'd demanded. And who was I to say no to him, right?

One thing for sure—I didn't know when it would happen, but I knew at some point in my life, I *would* be Mrs. Luke Murray, and as much as I wanted to wait for the right time, I was excited to know it would happen. Hey… maybe it would happen sooner than I thought.

Sidney

I couldn't even open my eyes fully. I had a splitting headache that was most likely brought on by the bottles of alcohol I'd been consuming every night since I heard about Faviola's death.

I still couldn't believe she was gone. I didn't want to believe it. I had no closure. Faviola's punk ass mama wouldn't even have a funeral for her because she couldn't get the money out of Tank to pay for the expenses. Even though Tank offered to pay for everything, he wasn't dumb enough to just cut Faviola's scamming ass mama a check, and that's why her mama ended up having her body cremated without even letting me see her one last time.

It was fucked up. Faviola had been my best friend, something like a sister, for as long as I'd even known what a friend was. I truly didn't know what I'd do without her. But on top of all that was my guilt. Faviola had called me to talk and I barely listened, formed opinions and then hung up on her and never called back. She needed me and I wasn't there.

"Sid... are you okay?"

As soon as I heard Mike's voice, I regretted answering the phone. The kiss we'd shared the other night... it would never happen again. I felt like he knew it because I'd been ignoring his calls and texts since it happened. I had a couple of days off so it was easy to avoid him... and then Faviola died.

"I'm alive," I answered Mike being honest. "I just can't understand it. I can't believe she would actually do this…"

"My sister committed suicide," Mike said, stunning me into silence for a few seconds.

"I didn't know you had a sister." Never since I'd known Mike had he mentioned that he had any siblings.

"No one here does. She died when she was in high school. I was in elementary. It was way before my family moved here. She was in love with her boyfriend and he cheated on her with another girl… wouldn't take her back no matter how much she begged him. She was devastated. We found her in the tub with her wrists slit. Her autopsy revealed that she was 6 weeks pregnant at the time."

I had fresh tears in my eyes by the time he was finished speaking. I wasn't one for all this crying shit, but I could hear the emotion in his voice and I knew he understood how it felt to lose someone the way I lost Faviola. Suicide left everyone alive feeling helpless to change something they knew they could have, had the person simply reached out before deciding to take their own life.

"She thought her life was over because she was pregnant by a man who didn't want her. She never even told us about the baby. We would've let her know that she was loved and the baby would be loved just the same. But…"

His voice cracked and I took the opportunity to take a deep breath and wipe the tears from my cheeks. Then there was a knock at my door and I jumped, not expecting any company.

"Thanks for calling me, Mike... and I'm really sorry about your sister."

"Don't mention it," Mike replied with a sigh. "I didn't tell you that for sympathy. I just wanted you to know I understand."

After hanging up with Mike, I ran to the door and peeked out to see who had been knocking. I can't lie... I nearly fell the fuck out when I saw who it was standing at the door.

"Tank?" I asked, snatching the door open.

He lifted his head and looked into my eyes. It was like he'd been run over by a tractor-trailer; worry lines ran all through his face, his eyes were swollen and red, and it looked like he hadn't shaved in days.

"Come in," I told him and stepped away from the door.

He moved to walk in and it was at that moment that I realized Yolo was standing behind him, off a little to the side. My heart did a triple beat and my stomach flip-flopped. In spite of our current situation, I couldn't help but notice that he looked so damn fine in his blue and white outfit. He had a fitted cap that sat low on his face, just barely showing his eyes. He looked up at me before moving, and the connection we had was still there. I knew just by looking at him what he was waiting for.

"You can come in too."

I turned away leaving Yolo to close and lock the door behind himself. I sat opposite Tank, who was in my only chair balancing his head on his hand and leaving Yolo and I to share the small loveseat. He sat down, not trying to push up on me, but it didn't matter. The loveseat was small enough for his thigh to still be pressed up against mine. I couldn't help but love the feel of it. Damn, I missed him.

"How did you find me?"

Tank cut his eyes to Yolo who, after a long pause, decided to speak up.

"I always knew where you were, Sid," he admitted. My eyes were still on Tank because I couldn't meet Yolo's eyes. His voice alone had my emotions in an uproar.

"I'll always know where you are no matter where you go and how far you run. Remember that."

My cheeks burned, and the part of my leg that was still touching Yolo seemed to get hot as well. My throat was dry so I cleared it but still couldn't speak. Luckily, Tank took over the conversation.

"I know you are... were Favi's best friend and you spoke to her before..." He paused not wanting to complete his sentence.

Before she killed herself, I mentally finished for him.

"I know you probably think I'm a fuck nigga for the things I've done, so I want to explain." He sighed deeply and I squinted my eyes at him, watching him intensely. What Tank didn't get is that I saw him as a brother. I couldn't blame him for anything that may have gone on between him and Faviola. He'd made some poor decisions on his end but so did she, because she knew the type of nigga he was from the beginning. He never changed. Still, it seemed like he wanted to get some things off his chest, so I allowed him to.

"I wasn't cheatin' on Favi. We weren't together—don't get me wrong, I had feelings for her but we hadn't gotten to the point of makin' shit official. I ain't wanna settle down… it had nothing to do with her, it was just me. When Nicole got pregnant, the only thing I could think about was I ain't wanna treat another chick like I did Favi while she was carrying my seed. Deep down, I feel like I stressed her into losing our baby…." His voice wavered and he took a deep breath. "So I didn't want that to happen again. I don't know if Nicole's baby is mine for sure, but I ain't wanna make her lose it by actin' an ass 'bout it. I decided to man up and be there for her. When Favi called me sayin' she was gon' kill herself because of Nicole, I thought she was on some bullshit but I drove over there anyways. She confronted me 'bout Nicole and some shit she'd heard… I ain't deny shit because I wasn't tryin' to hide shit! We wasn't together so why would I?"

He looked at me and paused, but I could tell he wasn't waiting for a real answer. I simply nodded my head for him to continue on.

"She tried to grab for my gun and we wrestled. She kept saying she was gon' kill herself. I got her to calm down… or so I thought, and I left. Wasn't until I was outside that I realized she'd gotten my gun back. I was about to walk back in the house when I heard the gunshot. I didn't even have to look inside to know she was gone. It was like I felt that shit in my soul."

My chest hurt. I didn't even know I was crying until I felt Yolo's arm wrap around me and him wiping the tears from my cheeks.

"You a'ight?" he asked me and I nodded my head.

"I just wanna know why she chose to do that when she had so many people here who love her. She called me earlier the day before and I never called her back. If I had…"

"It wouldn't have changed anything," Yolo cut in, squeezing my shoulders. "She had her mind made up about what she planned to do. One missed call doesn't void two plus decades of friendship, Sid. She knew you loved her and would be there for her, but she made that decision on her own. You aren't to blame for that shit. It's sad... but it ain't on you."

I wiped away more tears, knowing what he was saying was true. I'd been with Faviola through plenty of shit, fights that weren't mine to fight, drama that wasn't none of my business... there was no way she could believe I didn't love her or wouldn't be there for her. But still, she made the decision to leave all her problems behind by taking her own life.

"I don't blame you for anything, Tank," I told him, honestly. He looked at me with tear-filled eyes that were sparked with relief. I could see then that he'd come by because he needed to hear that I didn't blame him or hate him for what happened. I truly didn't.

"Thank you," he said.

"I never blamed you," I continued on. "You have always been who you are and... Favi knew that. I know this experience has changed you—maybe you'll understand that all the games should be over. If you want someone, make them yours. If you don't, leave them alone."

He pressed his lips together, ran his hand over the top of his head and nodded. Yolo stood and Tank did the same. My knees felt wobbly but with Yolo's help, I was able to escort them to the door.

"You gonna be alright?" He gazed right into my eyes, probing them deeply to be sure that my response would be an honest one.

"Yes, I'm good. Thanks for checking on me, Yolo."

He gave me a look like he wanted to say something and my heart started beating like a drum. And then, in the next second, it was like he changed his mind. Leaning over, he kissed me on the cheek and then backed away from the doorway.

"Lock up," was the last thing he said before he and Tank drove away.

***

Later that night, I was lying in the bed awake staring at the ceiling. There was no way I could sleep because I had too much bullshit on my mind. Carmella was in town and had invited me to her sister's office warming party, and although I wanted to see her and be around someone else I could call a friend, I couldn't bring myself to party so soon after losing both of my best friends: first Yolo and now Faviola.

After trying to find sleep for another hour, I did something I hadn't done in a very long time. I picked my ass up out the bed, got dressed and headed to Brooklyn. Nights like these, the basketball court was calling my name and I couldn't ignore it. So I stopped trying. I needed the release that shooting hoops alone on the court gave me. I needed to be active… stop lying around in the bed feeling sorry for myself.

But when I pulled up to the court, someone was already there. I could barely see him in the dark but I could pick up his outline under the dim streetlights. It was definitely Yolo. Like me, he probably couldn't sleep. I walked over to the entrance of the court and stepped through the gate. He turned around slowly, not even seeming surprised to see me.

"I figured you'd come out here," he said with his back to me, still dribbling the ball. "You wanna play one-on-one?" I nodded my head. "Okay, first to 21."

The game started and I played my hardest like I always did against Yolo, but the end result was the same. He beat my ass like I stole something, deciding at the end to finally start taking it easy on me.

"Stop playin' easy. I don't want no sympathy points." I was dead ass serious.

"I ain't takin' shit easy on you."

"Yes, you are!" I shouted, snatching the ball up into my arms and simultaneously pausing the game. "I know you enough to see that. I'm not a lil' ass girl, Yolo. And I don't need your fuckin' sympathy."

Yolo stared at me with big eyes. "Yo, you buggin' da fuck out right now."

Ignoring him, I shot the ball, sinking in a 3-point shot. Yolo shrugged and fell back in line to finish the game. I came up on him, decreasing the point spread but still lost. However, it was only by five points so I wasn't tripping.

"Aye, where you goin'?" Yolo asked me as I turned to walk away. The game was over and there was nothing left for me to say.

"Home."

"Not so fast." Yolo turned, sunk a shot and then walked over to me. "You said something earlier today. You said the games should be over and if you want someone to make them yours."

He reached out and lifted my face by pushing up on my chin. "You really believe that?" Speechless, I could only nod my head.

"Life's short, Sid. I fucked up with you a few times but my intentions for you—for us—have always been good. I'm tired of the games. I want you. I gave you your time but now I'm sick of that shit. You're the only one I want. You're the one I love."

Yolo bent down, lowering his lips until they met mine. When our lips connected, that's when the magic happened. It was crazy to me how being around Yolo took away all of my stress, sadness and fears. He gave me instant peace.

"I love you," he said, holding me close and pressing his body against mine. "You're my one."

"I love you, too." I replied. "And you'll forever be mine."

And then, before we could fall into our happily ever after, I was hit with the realization that everything was not settled between us. There was still one last thing I needed to tell Yolo and I prayed that he could forgive me... or at least spare me the same fate as LaTrese.

"Wait, I have something I have to say."

I pushed away from Yolo and he widened his eyes in shock, seeming a little panicked about what I was going to say.

"Let's sit down," I suggested. He wasted no time plopping down on the court and then passed me the ball so that I could sit on top of it.

After taking a deep breath, I rattled off everything I needed Yolo to know, making sure not to skip any details. It felt like the hardest thing I'd ever done in my life and the tears came almost immediately. I watched as his eyes widened in surprise when I told him about my pregnancy. I saw a glimmer of guilt when I mentioned finding out about him and LaTrese shortly after getting pregnant. And then there was the sadness that lingered when I detailed the abortion that my mama had forced on me.

"Why are you just now telling me this? Why did you keep it in all this time?"

The hurt in his voice was so heavy that my heart began to ache in my chest.

"I was angry at myself for being in love with you. And then I was ashamed at what my mama made me do. Eventually, I made myself forget all about it until what happened to LaTrese... I did the same thing she did and I was scared that—"

"You are not like LaTrese. Don't compare yourself to shit that bitch did!" he cut in angrily. "You're nothing like her. She killed her own child—"

"So did I!" I cried out, letting tears that I'd been holding flow freely.

"No, you didn't, and you better not ever say that shit again! You were a child. You were dealt a bullshit hand and you did what the fuck you had to do. It's not the fuckin' same."

Yolo stood up and walked over to me, kneeling down to wrap his arms around my body. He hugged me tightly as he softly kissed the tears away from my cheeks.

"Don't ever be scared to tell me shit. I don't care what it is," he said, rocking me gently. "Don't ever be afraid of me because no matter what happens, I'll never hurt you, Sid. Don't be afraid of me."

I wasn't and I wouldn't ever be.

Carmella

*S*ipping from my apple cider filled champagne glass, I watched Outlaw and Janelle together. They were the cutest couple in the room. I was truly happy for my sister because she deserved everything that was happening to her. She'd spent her childhood and most of her adulthood sacrificing her wants, being the responsible one and worrying about not letting anyone down. Now she was finally in a place where she was genuinely happy.

And I was jealous as hell.

Don't get me wrong: I was excited about the things going right for Janelle. Like truly excited. But her life was perfect and mine was... well, a mess. Thanks to my daddy, I would be back in school in the spring... all the way back in California though. I didn't want to be in L.A. anymore. I wanted to be in New York. I couldn't even get excited anymore about the atmosphere of L.A. and how it would help in my pursuit of transitioning from an Instagram model to a real deal model. I wasn't even sure I wanted to show my ass for the 'Gram anymore. The only thing I wanted was to be with Cree.

"Nice party but why all the fine niggas got a wifey? Like damn!" TreVonia asked. She walked up next to me with her hands on her shapely hips and her bottom lip poked out.

"Don't you have a man, Vonia?" I rolled my eyes but still had to smile a little. She was crazy as hell.

"I do," she admitted with a slick ass smile. "But he ain't here and ain't no harm in flirting or looking at another fine one. I got eyes, don't I?"

Giggling, I shook my head and looked across the room. Of course my eyes landed on Cree of all people. Shit! And he was looking so, so sexy too. He was standing right across the room from me, talking to his oldest brother, Kane, as he sipped on some brown liquid. He was definitely looking like a snack, and I would give everything to be able to eat his sexy ass up.

But I couldn't because he didn't want me. *Of course.*

"Well, Cree is single," I replied with a shrug. TreVonia rolled her eyes.

"That nigga is *not* single. Not with the way his ass been staring at you all night."

At me?

A dumbfounded expression crossed my face. TreVonia took one look at me and rolled her eyes like I was the stupidest person she'd ever seen, before stomping off. Before I knew it, my eyes were back on Cree again. This time he was looking directly at me and I completely froze. This was my first time laying eyes on him since he'd left Atlanta, and I hadn't had a conversation with him since he told me that I was being desperate. Maybe that was the reason my ass was about to break out in a cold sweat just from locking eyes with him.

While I tried to hold back on my panic attack, Cree continued to speak to his brother. They seemed to be having an intense conversation where Kane was doing most of the talking while Cree listened. The expression on Cree's face was sour but he still stood quietly, nodding his head while his older brother laid out the law.

"They are talking about you," a voice said from behind me. I turned around and found myself staring right into Teema's beautiful chocolate face.

"Who?" I asked her and she nodded her head towards Cree and Kane.

"They are. And I normally wouldn't interfere because I don't know you like that. But I can tell how much you like Cree, and I know how much of an asshole he can be."

I gulped down the rest of my apple cider and waved the glass for another one. As soon as the waiter brought it over, I gulped that one down too, just like it was real champagne. I didn't know Teema all that well and the way we met each other was not under the best of circumstances, but I felt like I could confide in her a little. She had a trusting face and she knew Cree longer than I did. I felt like she could give me some advice on how to deal with him.

"I love Cree... I swear I do. I've made mistakes but I've corrected them—not for him but for myself. And even though I've gotten my life back on track, I seriously can't see me living it without him in it. But he's just not feeling being with me right now." I finished what I had to say and dropped my head. This shit wasn't like me. Niggas were usually beating down the door to get me to pay them a lil' bit of attention but instead, here I was about to cry because I couldn't have Cree.

"Cree is stubborn to the point of being stupid. Right now he calls himself punishing you. But I know him. He's also possessive about what he feels is his. As soon as he thinks you're not available to kiss his ass, he'll come around. The shit he does is stupid and Kane's telling him that right now. If you don't believe me when it comes to him, try calling another nigga to come up here and pick you up. See what happens."

Teema winked at me before walking away and leaving me to think on what she'd just said.

Was Cree really that damn petty? I asked myself, but it didn't take long for the answer to pop right into my head. *Of course he was!*

I didn't have anybody I could call to come up and grab me without having expectations of me that I wouldn't want to fulfill. The last thing I wanted was to be caught up having to entertain a nigga just because this little plan with Cree didn't work. But then an idea came to mind and I shot off a quick text.

About thirty minutes later, my ride was in front of Janelle's building dressed in a nice ass white sports coat, blue jeans fitted just right to show off his nice physique, white sneakers and a fitted cap pulled down low over his face, looking too damn good. The front of Janelle's building was all glass so you could see out from the inside, and everyone was casting curious glances at the mystery man standing near the passenger side of his creamy new Benz.

"Well, that's my ride," I said loud enough for most of the room to hear. Then I walked over to Janelle and my daddy, kissing them both on the cheek to say goodbye. Out of the corner of my eye, I saw Cree staring in my direction but I ignored him.

"Stay safe, baby girl. I'll see you before I fly out in the morning…

that is, unless you changed your mind and want to go with me."

I shook my head, hoping everything would go right tonight and I wouldn't want to be on the next thing smoking back to Atlanta.

As soon as my back was turned and I began to walk away, I took a deep breath and prayed that this plan of Teema's would work. She caught my eye on the way out and winked. I returned her expression of courage with a lop-sided smile of my own—one that mirrored my conflicting feelings—and walked on. I had my hand on the handle of the door when I felt someone grab me on my side.

"You're leavin'?"

My heart squeezed tight in my chest. I knew his voice... didn't even have to turn around to know it was him.

"Yeah, my ride is waiting for me," I replied back with ease. I turned around but still did not look Cree in his eyes. I was trying to keep my head together.

"Who dis new nigga you 'bout to roll out with, Mel? That's how it is with me and you now? This how we treat each other? Just have new niggas poppin' up at the spot?" Cree narrowed his focus on me, making me feel intimidated under his stare. Still, I kept my composure.

"Why you so concerned? You don't want me!"

"Da *fuck* you mean?" he shot back through gritted teeth. A few people standing nearby gasped and stared in our direction. "Da fuck kinda shit you on right now, Mel?"

Wait... what?!

Okay, game over. Now I was really getting pissed off. How could

Cree stand in my face acting like I was in the wrong for fake moving on, after he'd made it clear that he wasn't interested in being with me?

"What are you talkin' about? You told me—"

"Fuck all that bullshit I said and hear what da fuck I'm sayin'!" I snapped my neck back at his tone. "You ain't goin' *nowhere* with that nigga!"

"Excuse me? You can't tell me what to do!"

I was truly irritated. Forget about this being all part of a plan. Cree was getting on my damn nerves with his bipolar ass.

"I *can* tell you what to do because I *am* your man. Ain't shit changed! We was just on break."

Break? This nigga was buggin'.

"Well, we can stay on break because I'm tired of your muthafuckin' games." All the hood I never thought I had was coming out of me. "You know damn well you told me there was no 'us.' Now get out of my way and let me go!"

Cree recoiled as if I'd shot him with my words. I cut my eyes at him one last time and then swiveled around on the balls of my feet to leave.

But he stopped me... again.

"Mel, don't leave me. The past few months have been torture for me without you. And I know I been actin' stupid but I ain't never thought we was actually over. I just had to be sure that you was good without me makin' you good, know what I mean?"

"No." I crossed my arms in front of my chest, kicked my hip to the side and looked him square in his eyes.

"What I mean is that I wanted to make sure that once I brought you back into my life, you wouldn't let all the bullshit I'm in affect you in the same way, and get you back using. I felt like maybe bein' with a nigga like me was pushin' you down the wrong path. I survive from the streets and you a college girl... was a college girl before you met me. You got with me and your life went crazy. I had to be sure that you got back on track before I tried to pull you back in. I was being careful with this shit the only way I knew how."

Finally understanding what he was saying, I shook my head profusely.

"Cree, I was already spiraling out of control *before* I met you. And yes, my usage increased but that was on me, not you. I was using to cope with my job and the stupid decisions I made concerning school. When I got here, I was already failing out of school and I came here with the intentions on getting that bullshit job. My best friend warned me about working with Zeke and I didn't listen... so see, none of this was because of you or your lifestyle. I was already fucked up."

Dropping his gaze to the floor, Cree nodded his head a little and digested what I said. Then he lifted his head and let his eyes meet mine. A small smirk crossed his face.

"I'm glad you were already fucked up. At least I ain't have nothin' to do with that shit," he gloated.

I rolled my eyes at his rude ass. Did I really want this man?

"Did you mean what you said about us still being together or was that just more lies to get what you want out of me?"

He squinted his eyes at me and scrunched up his nose in a frown. "I wouldn't lie to you 'bout shit like that. I never saw us as not together. I was just tryin' to get you to focus on you and your recovery. You wasn't away long and I wasn't sure you were really over all that shit. The party lifestyle and all. But I been watchin' you and I trust you."

I bit down on my smile, hoping that I was hiding how damn happy I was. A kid in a candy store ain't have shit on me. It was official.

"Okay well… let me just tell my friend that he can go," I told Cree when I remembered that I had someone outside waiting on me.

"Naw, let me tell that nigga where he can take his ass." Cree started towards the door and I panicked, grabbing his arm.

"No!"

"Back up," he said and shook me off with ease.

I watched as his other hand went to his side, and I found myself praying to God that he didn't have a gun. But what the hell was I thinking? Of course his crazy ass had a gun! My mind in severe panic-mode, I ran outside behind Cree, trying to stop anything from happening before it got started.

"Aye, nigga, what's up? You here tryin' to scoop up my ole lady?"

Cree rolled up on the man standing beside the Mercedes Benz like a straight goon. I heard some commotion behind me and turned around in time to see Outlaw, Tank and Kane rolling out the door, posted up and ready to go, if necessary.

"Listen, nigga," the man started, lifting his head. "I don't want no problems from yo' punk ass. I'm just comin' here to grab my bitch so we can hit the muthafuckin' club and drop that shit like it's hoooooooot!"

I almost snorted out a laugh when I saw the quizzical and stunned expression on Cree's face. It wasn't until the man took the hat off his head that a smile crossed Cree's face and I burst out laughing.

"Man, this some bullshit!" Cree yelled out and I couldn't hold my laughter any longer.

"Did I do a good job with that thug shit? I know I couldn't carry it the whole way through but I was convincing at the beginning, right?" Bryan asked as I nearly doubled over laughing. "Call me Baby Thug. I got dat juice!"

Shaking my head, I peered at Bryan through the tears in my eyes. "Bry, don't evaaaa say that shit again!"

"Aye, bruh, I guess you got this shit, huh?" Outlaw asked with a smirk on his face, obviously enjoying the show. Tank and Kane had already gone back inside once they saw Bryan was no real threat to anyone.

"Yeah, they on some fuckin' games right now," Cree told him, still shaking his head at the sudden turn of events.

"Carm, you still need me to stay or you with yo' boo tonight?" Bryan asked and I smiled, ducking my head a little to the side. A dead giveaway as to what I had in mind.

"We gotta get together this week but tonight I'm goin' to stay with the boo, if you don't mind."

He nodded his head and leaned over to kiss me on the cheek before walking around to the driver's side of his car. Once Bryan drove off, I turned to look at Cree, trying to hide the smirk on my face.

"So you got all jealous about Bryan, huh?"

I started to laugh but Cree didn't find shit funny. Bending over, he grabbed me and hoisted me over his shoulder, leaving my ass hanging in the air by his head. I kicked out my legs for him to put me down, but he only held me tighter and spanked my ass like I was his child.

"I told you I was gon' beat yo' ass 'bout playin' with me, Mel," he told me as I squealed out in laughter.

My ass was in the air, probably exposed as he walked me over to his car, but I didn't give a damn. I had my man back, and I'd be damned if I messed this up ever again.

Epilogue

*T*he crisp smell of jasmine blew in the air as birds chirped their witness of how beautiful of a day it was. The sun was high, but there was a gentle breeze that provided relief to all the guests as they flowed into the chapel. Inside the chapel, Kane stood with his thick brows knotted in worry as he looked around the packed church, wondering if the crowd could see the thoughts racing through his mind.

"She's not coming," he said, before letting out a short burst of air. It felt like it was all he had left in his lungs. "She's not... I know it."

"She is," Cree assured him, but his face did not follow his words. His lips were pulled into a straight line and his brows were bunched together like was natural for someone who was struggling to make their mouth say something their mind didn't believe.

"Don't sweat it, fam. She's coming," Luke affirmed once again. "She's just late. It's only been twenty minutes. I should kick her ass for bein' on CP time tho."

"She late as hell but she's comin'," Yolo added. Tank walked up with a chicken bone in his mouth. Obviously, he'd already taken it upon himself to dip into the reception food before the ceremony had even gotten a chance to start.

"Stop actin' crazy, nigga. You know Teema is comin'. Calm da fuck down," he voiced in between chomping on the chicken wing.

Kane shook his head, pushing away his brothers' words the instant they said them.

"No... she's not late. That's not like her. She's never late for shit."

"Yo, if this is what it's like to be married, I'on know if I want that shit," Luke said, cutting his eyes at Kane. "Got niggas actin' like a bitch and shit."

Before Kane could respond with the fist he'd balled up by his side, the doors of the church opened and everyone turned towards the sound. The sunlight burst in, temporarily blinding Kane from seeing whom it was standing before him. But then his eyes adjusted and his heart filled with a joyous feeling that he never knew he could feel. She was there.

There at the front of the church stood Teema, dressed like an angel. Her hair fell in loose curls around her shoulders and a hibiscus flower hung near her ear. She was the perfect picture of beauty, style, and grace. Everything that he needed in his life. His heart swelled in his chest as he stared at the only woman who had his heart. The one he would love to vow his life to... forever.

"She purrrrty," Luke teased, jabbing Kane in the side.

Cree, Yolo, and Tank nodded in agreement, each of them happy for their brother, but thinking about their own women: Cree was thinking about Carmella, Yolo was thinking about Sidney, and Tank... Tank was thinking about a woman that he'd just started to date—wasn't sure where it would go, but he felt like he wanted to make it official. After feeling the guilt that hadn't yet left him after Faviola's suicide, he vowed that he would change his love life for the better and start acting like the grown ass man he was. The new woman in his life demanded that after all.

"I now pronounce you husband and wife," Janelle said, looking from Kane to Teema who hadn't taken their eyes off each other for the entire ceremony. "You may kiss the bride."

When Kane grabbed his new wife and pulled her into a deep embrace, Luke took the opportunity to grab Janelle and kiss her as well.

"Luke!" she gasped, smacking him on the shoulder once he'd let her go. "That is sooo inappropriate! This is not our wedding!"

"It could've been but you playin' around with a nigga heart," was Luke's only reply. He smiled at the disgusted look on Janelle's face, completely unfazed by her response.

One of these days she'll realize who the hell she's dealing with, he thought to himself before blowing her a kiss and reaching out to rub her round belly. She smacked his hand away but all it made him do was laugh. Every single day of their lives, she made him the happiest man on Earth.

In the past few months, Janelle hadn't changed her mind about getting married before her career took off but Luke knew it was coming soon. The week after she told him they had a baby on the way, he bought her a multi-million dollar estate that made the place she'd grown up in look like a shack used to house slaves. True to his style, he was not to be outdone by any muthafucka when it came to Janelle—and that included her father.

After initially refusing to move in with him, Janelle gave in as soon as she laid eyes on the house. Luke had spared no expense, and it was obvious he'd picked the house with her in mind. She had an office so that she could work from home, a nursery that rivaled something put together for a celebrity's seed, and many other rooms specifically decorated just for her to enjoy—even a room specifically for her to watch *Scandal* in with photos of Olivia Pope all over the walls, along with some of her most famous sayings—'It's handled' being Janelle's favorite.

The more Janelle thought about it, she was already living the life of Mrs. Murray...all that was left was to make it official. She hadn't told Luke yet, but she already had a date in mind for the wedding and was now determined to make sure they tied the knot before their baby girl was born.

As Teema and Kane walked out of the chapel, hand in hand, the groomsmen and bridesmaids walked down behind them. Cree and Carmella smiled at each other before grabbing each other's hands. Cree tucked Carmella's body in close to him and felt a flutter in his chest that he had been feeling more often than not when he looked at her and they locked eyes.

She's the one.

The past few days those three words had been cycling through his mind and he knew it was true. He knew that Carmella was the one, and he knew that he needed to follow after his brothers Outlaw and Kane and put a ring on her finger. But the stubborn side of him couldn't see asking Carmella to be his so soon. Unlike his brothers, Cree wasn't the one to take the plunge so fast and preferred to date Carmella just a little bit longer before locking her down. It wasn't just because of the man he was; it was also because of the woman she was. She loved her freedom just about as much as she loved him. He knew that it wasn't the time to lock her down.

On the good side, she was attending school in New York instead of Los Angeles, a decision she'd made on her own so that she could be close to him. What she didn't know is that whether she transferred schools or not, they would have been together because if she hadn't, he had been prepared and ready to move to Cali in order to be with her.

At the reception, Teema tossed the bouquet with a certain lady's name in mind, and that same woman was the one who caught it. Sidney hadn't even been really trying to participate and was only even standing in the vicinity of the bouquet toss because of Carmella's urgings, but when the flowers landed right inside of her open palms, she couldn't help but smile and cut her eyes at Yolo, who was staring at her with a love-struck expression on his face. No love was perfect and theirs was definitely anything but that, but it was true, it was honest, and it was forever.

Tank fingered the newest charm that he wore at the end of his gold link chain. It was the letter 'F' for Faviola and every time he looked at it, he was reminded of her and the promise that he made to himself that he would never play with a woman's emotions in the way that he'd played with hers. Truth be told, Tank did feel like he loved Faviola, and he felt like he could have settled down with her, but his need to always have more than what he needed became a curse that was hard to shake. And, eventually, yielding to those selfish desires cost him when Faviola decided to take her own life.

Tank had been minding his own business at Janelle's office warming party when he met a woman who stole his interest in a way none other ever had before. It wasn't just the fact that she was beautiful—although she was—and it wasn't the fact that she was smart—even though she was incredibly intelligent, too—but it was the fact that she had a spark about her that resonated deep within him the moment they locked eyes.

Tank didn't even know that Mixie was Janelle's sister; he had no idea how they even knew each other or why she'd been invited to the party, but he made up in his mind that he would ask her out, and he *would* be a good man to her if she gave him the chance to be. The good news was that she did give him the chance and he'd been working at being a better man every day since. They'd only been official for a couple months so far, but Tank had to say that he was really enjoying riding the 'one woman only' train along with his brothers. Maybe being in love was all people claimed it to be.

"Get your big belly ass over here, Janelle!" Luke yelled, earning a frown from Janelle before she walked towards him with her mouth poked out. "The hell you trying to catch the damn bouquet for? I done put a muthafuckin' ring on yo' finger already and dropped a baby in yo' gut but you still don't wanna marry a nigga. You don't deserve the bouquet or none of that other shit I done gave you. Go sit'cho big stomach ass down!"

If Janelle had been a few shades lighter, her cheeks would have shown ruby red from embarrassment. Everyone nearby howled in laughter at his words, but she only grunted and turned her nose in the air as she walked in the opposite direction. *Waddled* in the opposite direction was more like it, seeing as she was eight months pregnant but really looked like she was around twenty months.

"I'm just playin' wit' yo' ass. Stop takin' shit so serious," Luke apologized, grabbing her by the hand. He pulled hard, tugging her just enough so that she turned in his direction.

"You forgive me?"

It was hard for Janelle to stop the smile from cracking through on her lips when she saw the pouty face that accompanied his question. No matter what he did, she would always love this man and would always forgive him.

"No, I don't," she replied, but Luke knew the truth.

"When you gon' marry me though? For real?" he asked her with all seriousness in his tone.

For some reason, her wearing his ring wasn't enough. Even the fact that she lived in the house he'd bought for her and was about to have his baby wasn't enough. He wanted Janelle to have his last name. He wanted to feel like she was really his. He felt like his greatest accomplishment in life would be the moment she became his wife. It was crazy to him how the woman he thought he would hate when he first laid eyes on her in the courtroom, was the woman that he couldn't see himself living without.

"Luke…" Janelle started, her words dying off as she wondered if she should go ahead and tell him what she'd been thinking. She wanted it to be a surprise, but she should have known that wouldn't work well with Luke. When it came to him, things rarely went according to plan.

"I decided that I want to get married before the baby comes..."

It was all Janelle had to say. Bending down, Luke held her tightly in his arms and kissed her like he didn't know they weren't the only ones in the room. He was actually well aware that they weren't, he just couldn't bring himself to care.

"The way you just tongued a nigga down got me second-guessing if I really wanna get my golds put back in," Luke teased once they broke their embrace. "You gon' still kiss a nigga like that if I do?"

Janelle grimaced her disgust. "Ew, no. I won't be kissing you with that yuck mouth."

"Yo' ass was doin' a lot more than kissin' this yuck mouth back in the day," Luke reminded her with a cocky smile.

He walked away to chill with his brothers for a little while, leaving Janelle thinking back to the very beginning of when they met. It was insane to her whenever she thought about how they became the couple they were. Back then when she was Janelle Alexandria Elizabeth-Ann Pickney, the oldest of four girls, graduate of New York Law School, two years earlier than expected, at the top of her class and the apple of her father's eye, no one could ever have convinced her she would fall in love with one of the most dangerous men in all of New York City.

"I guess that's why they say 'we make plans and God laughs,'" she muttered under her breath as she shook her head and took one last look at her man, and husband to be, turning up with his brothers. They had red cups in the air and, from the looks of it, Cree was rolling up a fresh blunt for them to puff on the balcony. Janelle snickered to herself when Luke caught her eye and seductively licked out his tongue at her before walking outside behind the other Murrays.

She had planned every step of her entire life but never would she have thought she would fall in love with an Outlaw... until she did.

THE END!

MAKE SURE TO LEAVE A REVIEW!

Text PORSCHA to 25827
to keep up with Porscha's latest releases!

To find out more about her, visit www.porschasterling.com

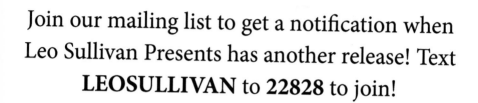

Join our mailing list to get a notification when Leo Sullivan Presents has another release! Text **LEOSULLIVAN** to **22828** to join!

To submit a manuscript for our review, email us at <u>leosullivanpresents@gmail.com</u>

Get LiT!

Download the LiT app today and enjoy exclusive content, free books, and more!

CPSIA information can be obtained
at www.ICGtesting.com
Printed in the USA
LVOW10s1630270218
568056LV00005B/992/P

9 781946 789075